Enjoy!

D. S.

INSURGENT FIRE

BY
D.S. CANNON

For you. Thank you for being a part of this journey.

TABLE OF CONTENTS

FIRST CONTACT

September 14th, 2008

Panjwayi District, Afghanistan

The shade of the Light Armored Vehicle felt cool as Henry climbed into the back. It was a noticeable difference from the scorching desert heat outside, but it was still enough to break a sweat. He moved into the vehicle, shoving an ammo-can out of the way with his foot. Dusting off the blast blanket, he sat down in the same seat he had sat in for the last two years of training. It has come to be known as 'Henry's seat'. He began his pre-road-move mental checklist; ensure weapon was on safe, make sure magazine pouches are secure on vest, adjust helmet, adjust ass in his seat and light a smoke. After a couple of calming drags on his cigarette, he leaned forward and prepared a playlist on his iPod. The iPod wheel clicked through the speakers as Henry scrolled for the perfect song.

Henry Carson was an average Canadian. He was the kind of guy you walk past on the street and don't give a second thought about. He grew up in a military family. His father was a Sergeant, so they moved around a lot, but he never struggled to make friends. He was a strong student and his goal was always to attend University. Somewhere away from home, but not so far that he couldn't come home for some of mom's holiday turkey. He was a scientist at heart and had an overwhelming interest in biology. He wanted to know what made people work, why some people could not walk, and why some were born differently. All of the fascinating things that made the body work. But, there he was, twenty-two years old and sitting in the back of an armored vehicle, armed to the teeth, as part of the Canadian contingent in Afghanistan.

Henry was nervous, but his composure suggested otherwise. He sat there calmly in the back corner of the vehicle, his right leg bouncing in light agitation. Close enough to the beat of the music from his iPod that no one would interpret it differently. The platoon Henry was part of, the one he spent a year and a half training with, waited to depart the main camp at Kandahar Air Field and head to the patrol base where they would live for the next several months. Soldiers hurried about the vehicle yard with cans of ammo, boxes of food and jerry cans of water.

As Henry sat there, playing with the sling on his rifle, he used his index finger on his free hand to clean dust from his weapons holographic sight. He began to think back to the briefing they received on where the recent Improvised Explosive Device activity had been in the past thirty days, and how it had largely been centralized on the route they planned to take. Suddenly a thought hit him. What if our vehicle hits an IED? What if I die? Fuck! He thought to himself, trying his hardest to hide his fear. I'll never see IRON-MAN 2! He thought. Looking around at the faces of his friends, Henry quickly realized the absurdity of that thought, and cleared his throat.

"It feels like we've been sitting here for fucking hours!" Maxwell shouted while pounding the roof of the vehicle with a clenched, fist. He was clearly not hiding his nerves and agitation as well as Henry.

"Quit being a bitch," retorted Tremblay, as he climbed up the ramp and stood up into the air sentry hatch.

"It has been a while, like, an hour or so… I think," Henry said in a half-assed attempt to calm Maxwell down.

Private Joshua Maxwell was only nineteen and had joined the Army right out of high school. He was a short, stocky person with a typical 'Jar-Head' style haircut. His plans were to be a career soldier, so he tried his hardest. Sometimes he would try a little too hard. He was constantly getting in the way and would always manage to fuck things up during training. Once, during a live fire exercise, Maxwell forgot the bolt from his rifle back in the weapons vault. Without a bolt, the rifle was essentially a ten-pound metal club with plastic accessories. Max hid his mistake well too. He managed not to fire a shot during the four-hour ordeal. Even when clearing rooms and shooting pop-up targets during the counter-attack phase he managed to hide his epic fuck-up from his section mates and the range safety staff. Henry didn't think anything of it until the range staff came to clear their weapons. That's when Max admitted he was missing his bolt. At first, he felt embarrassed for Max when the Range Safety Officer, a random large-statured Sergeant who hated his life, started to scream at him for being a 'colossal fucking moron'. But when the Sergeant yelled that Max could have gotten his fire-team partner killed, Henry realized the severity of the situation. Shit, that's me! He thought. So, Henry couldn't blame Max for being a little nervous; after all, they did just receive a two-hour briefing on where they might die, and this time, real lives were on the line.

"Pass me the LMG, Doc," Tremblay shouted down to the medic while fixing his goggles. The second oldest person in the section was Jonathan

Tremblay. He was in his mid-thirties, still a Corporal and had no family back home. He was what they called a 'Corporal-for-life'. He was happy to just be a grunt, do what he's told and get paid doing it. As long as it involved guns, explosions, or inappropriate jokes, Tremblay was happy. Like Max, Tremblay was a career soldier; the difference between them was that Tremblay didn't have to try. He was just naturally good at his job.

Doc Taylor passed the Light Machine Gun up through the hatch, hitting Tremblay in the nuts in the process.

"I fucking hate you Doc," Tremblay said through the pain and clenched teeth.

"No, you fucking love me, and you know it," Doc Taylor replied. Tremblay smiled at Doc with a cheesy grin and blew him a kiss.

"Hey Sergeant! When are we fucking leaving?" a voice said over the vehicle's intercom.

Henry reached over and grabbed the microphone where Sergeant Howard usually sits, pressing the talk button.

"He's just coming now, looks like we might be moving out soon," Henry said into the mic.

"'Bout fucking time!" Max said in relief.

Sergeant James Howard climbed up the ramp of the LAV and stood up into the empty air sentry hatch next to Tremblay. Henry passed him the headset and microphone he had just finished speaking into. Sergeant Howard strapped the headset on and lit a cigarette, taking a long haul off it and nearly finishing it in one go. He pressed the talk switch and took a deep breath. "Alright gents," Howard said over the intercom, "We have to make a small detour on route."

"What kind?" The voice from before replied in frustration.

"The kind where we need to assist an American convoy who just found an IED, Heart!" Howard yelled, "So you just drive when I say drive, got it!"

"Yes Sarge," Private Heart, the owner of the voice replied over the intercom from the drivers hatch.

"All call signs three, this is three one, we're Oscar Mike," the platoons Commanding Officer said over the main radio.

Oscar Mike, a phrase meaning 'On the Move'. Most soldiers loved it. Henry hated it. He hated it to the point where he would grit his teeth whenever someone said it.

"RAMP CLEAR!" Tremblay shouted. The sound of the ramp's hydraulics hissed like something from a science fiction movie, followed by a heavy clunk. The sound of the twin turbo Cat engine whistled loudly from the engine compartment just a few feet from Henry's head. It reminded him of steam escaping a pipe. They all slid a few inches in their seats as they roared away from camp, in part of a four LAV convoy off to provide extra security for the American convoy just a few klicks west.

Once the convoy was through the main gate the LAV gunner, Private Jason Field, unlocked the turret and began scanning the surroundings for suspicious activity. As the turret swung by the drivers hatch, Field tossed an empty water bottle into the compartment bouncing it off the back of Hearts' head. "I'll turn this car around," Heart shouted from the drivers hatch.

***

After an hour of weaving through the congested streets of Kandahar City, the convoy arrived at the Americans location. Sergeant Howard told the section to stay in the LAV and keep watch, while he met with the American troops and other section commanders. Tremblay sat down and said that his legs were getting tired from standing. He asked Henry to take over his watch in the air sentry hatch, so he could make some coffee in their 'non-regulation' percolator.

While standing there, Henry took in all the sights of the landscape. He realized how green the country actually is. There were a mix of grape and marijuana fields as far as he could see. However, the only other colour was brown. The brownish-tan colour of dried mud. Walls, buildings, grape rows, all made of mud. It's actually kind of nice, Henry thought to himself, as he starred into the distance. Every few minutes he would adjust his stance, so he could overhear the meeting with the Americans. He didn't learn much, except that no one was hurt. The meeting was brief, and once informed of the situation, the Canadian sections commanders made their way back to their vehicles. Sergeant Howard briefed Henry and the rest of Three One Charlie on the IED location, that no one was hurt and that they had it under control.

"As soon as the Engineers complete a controlled detonation, we are out of here," He said. "So everybody stay down." Tremblay closed the air-sentry hatches and sat quietly sipping his coffee.

"All call signs three, this is three one, detonation in 3…2…1…" The force of the explosion from the IED shook the near seventeen tonne vehicle. After a couple of seconds, debris came raining down on the roof of the LAV. Tremblay waited for the dirt rain to stop before he opened his air sentry hatch again. When he did, dust started to flow into the vehicle, inciting a few coughs. A voice on the radio squawked an all clear signal and the Canadian convoy began to move on, headed for their final destination.

**

As the LAV convoy pulled into their new home, Outpost Nal, Henry noticed the outgoing troops already mounted up and ready to leave, with the exception of two soldiers, one in the north tower, and one in the south. The outpost was an old Taliban compound that the Canadians reclaimed during an attack. Hesco walls and sandbags now surrounded the compound, with two towers added for watch to the North and South. It was a drab looking place. The brown of the Hesco walls topped with the green of sandbags. The only other colour was the red and white Canadian Flag. Sergeant Howard poked his head down from the hatch and ordered Henry and Tremblay to relieve the two in the towers. Here we go... thought Henry. Apart from the ride, this was the first time he was stepping foot 'Outside the Wire'. The couple of seconds it took Henry to get up and move towards the back of the vehicle felt like an eternity. His heart already pounding as though he just finished a hundred metre sprint. Henry and Tremblay took a couple deep breaths. Tremblay grabbed the switch to lower the LAV ramp, looked over at Henry and nodded to confirm that he was good to go. Henry nodded back. The heavy ramp lowered, crashing to the ground, crushing the rocks underneath as if they were made of chalk. As they exited the LAV, Henry went left, Tremblay went right, as they have hundreds of times throughout training.

They sprinted towards the outpost gate with everything they had.

Mostly out of fear. Fear that they might be the first casualties in the platoon. As they ran, the dirt kicked up all around them creating a small cloud of dust. The sand was so fine it was like running through baby powder. Once they were inside the outpost, they changed their sprint to a slight jaunt and each headed to a tower. Small puffs of baby-powder-like sand kicking off their heels as they went.

As Henry climbed the steps to the South Tower, he couldn't help but notice the spent casings lying all around and a small wave of fear crashed over him. A fear that maybe he made a mistake in coming here. "Looks like you boys have seen some shit, eh?" Henry said as he climbed the last few steps into the tower. His foot kicked some brass casings out of the way, knocking them into the grooves of the plywood flooring.

"What gave it away?" The soldier replied acrimoniously. Henry was quick to pick up on the soldier's bitter tone and brushed it off. It was apparent to Henry that this guy just wanted to go home. From the looks of the place, they had a busy stint in the outpost. As Henry walked up next to the soldier, his eyes drifted up to the beams in the tower. The thick cross beams riddled with bullet holes and splintered at the back. He choked down a large wad of spit that formed in his mouth, in a classic cartoon gulp fashion.

"Yeah, took some machine gun fire a couple nights ago," the soldier said following Henry's gaze upwards to the bullet holes. "Not as bad as that though," he said, pointing to the North Tower. Henry looked over next to the stairs that Tremblay was climbing. In the wall, a massive hole, recently patched with sandbags.

"What happened?" Henry asked. A look of worry on his face.

"Took an RPG. Fucked the boys in the tower up pretty good."

"Shit, sorry to hear man," Henry said, his gaze still caught by the damage. After shaking his head clear and removing his tactical vest, Henry questioned the soldier on his arcs of fire, the state of the machine guns and if there were any areas of interest that he should pay particular attention. The soldier pointed out a big marijuana field to the southwest stating that the Taliban love to fire from there, as well as the long ditch one hundred metres to their front.

"Thanks…. Take it easy," Henry said waving at the soldier with two fingers on his right hand.

"Git some," the soldier replied, walking down the stairs.

***

A long and uneventful month had passed, and Henry's platoon had officially settled into their new home. They had an established routine of tower shifts, patrols, and cooking. Everything seemed to flow perfectly. Henry and the rest of Charlie section had just finished their week of patrols, and they were glad to be on tower duty. A welcomed break from all the walking. They had found a few IED's over the last week, but luckily, they were able to spot them before they detonated. An American UH-60 Black Hawk helicopter had dropped some supplies off along with some juicy steaks for the platoon. Alpha section was on cooking duty this week, so they dove right in to the steaks getting them ready for dinner when Bravo returned from patrolling.

The platoon still had yet to see any combat, and some of the guys were starting to get a little restless. There were a few firefights between the Afghan National Army and the Taliban in a nearby village that got their blood pumping, but that was it. During a mid-afternoon shift, Sergeant Howard did the rounds to see how his troops were making out at their posts. Max and Henry were together in the South Tower chatting about their plans for when they returned home. Max was going to apply for his leadership course, and Henry wanted to go to school.

"Coffee, boys?" Sergeant Howard asked, holding two cups out.

"Thanks Sarge," Max replied. They both reached over and took a cup from Howard. He began to check over the weapons while the boys sipped on their coffee.

"I've told you about the Crack-Thump, right?" He asked.

"Many times," Henry replied.

"No, what's that?" Max asked.

"It's the sound of being shot at," Howard replied, turning inwards towards them. "The 'Crack' is the sound of the bullet breaking the sound barrier over your head," he said using his index finger to motion above his head.

"And the thump?" Max said, with a worried look on his face.

"The thump is the sound of the gun firing."

"Oh, weird…" Max said shaking his fear as if everything was all right now. Henry began to think back to his time spent training for deployment. He thought about how they don't really teach you what it's like to be shot at. Which is probably for the best.

As Sergeant Howard descended the tower stairs, some distant movement caught Henry's eye. He grabbed the binoculars and began to observe a man in the marijuana field about four hundred metres to the southwest. He looked like a simple farmer wearing typical Pashtun dress consisting of white linen clothes, a brown vest and a red Peshawari cap.

Henry pointed him out to Max, and Max moved in behind the machine gun, his hand trembling the slightest amount. It was the first time in a month they had seen any movement that wasn't a vehicle traveling up or down the dried up Arghendab river. The man didn't appear to be carrying anything with him, so Henry and Max continued to observe.

Henry passed the binoculars to Max and walked over to the field phone mounted to the wall. A phone with a direct line downstairs to the platoon command post. He was going to call down and let them know there was movement. "Hey…hey…hey…hey…." Max said nervously. "There's four other guys with him now."

"Lemme see," Henry said. He hung up the phone and walked back to the wall, grabbing the binoculars from Max's outstretched hand. Just as he focused on the now five males in the field, he could make out what appeared to be an AK-47 in one of their hands, the male in the red Peshawari cap, raising it up towards the outpost. "What…the fuck…." Henry said inquisitively. Suddenly they heard it. The sound they had heard so much about, but never actually heard before. The 'Crack-Thump'. It reminded Henry of being on the range only this version of the sound was different. It was deadly.

CRACK! Thump CRACK! Thump CRACK! Thump

"CONTACT!" a voice screamed from the north. Tremblay was scrambling to move his machine gun, so he could fire over the outpost to the south.

"FUCK!" screamed Max as he shakily aimed the machine gun and fired off a long burst. It seemed so surreal to Henry. The majority of the incoming rounds were falling short, and Henry watched as they kicked up rocks and dust. The motion of the skipping rocks and puffs of dirt entranced Henry. A round slammed into the already splintered crossbeam inches above Henry's head, quickly knocking him out of his trance. It was a hollow thudding sound. He ducked. The sounds of Max and Tremblay returning fire from their machine guns were deafening. His ears ringing during every lull in gunfire. Henry grabbed his rifle and joined the fight. He began firing into the field where the insurgents were, but they were ducking in and out, making it difficult to take a clear shot. He barely noticed the recoil of his rifle in his shoulder over the adrenaline pumping through his body.

"LOADING!" Max screamed, as he opened another can of 7.62 millimetre ammo for the machine gun.

"COVERING!" Henry yelled, returning a faster volley of semi-automatic fire. Suddenly, over all the gunfire there was a sound Henry had definitely never heard before. A sickening wet thud echoed through the tower, like someone slapping a pool of water. Henry felt a warm spray on his face. He fucking spit on me! Henry thought. As he turned to yell at Max, he saw his body slump over to the floor, with the ammo still in his hands. A round had hit Max just below the left eye, piercing his head and exiting out the back, painting the wall behind them looked like a scene decorated for a haunted house. "WHAT THE FUCK!" Henry screamed in terror, "MAX IS HIT!" he yelled over his shoulder.

Doc Taylor came sprinting up the stairs with his medical bag. He crouched down next to Max and began to examine him. Henry continued to return fire with his rifle with a quick burst of automatic fire. By this time, the patrolling section was moving into a flanking position on the eastern side of the field, and the cooking section had taken up firing positions along the wall; dressed in their body armor, boots and boxer shorts. To Tremblay, the display of firepower was amazing. He began to cheer as he cut down an insurgent with his machine gun. Unfortunately, no one else had any idea what had just happened to Max.

An explosion from behind them shook the tower as the sounds of shrapnel twanged all around them. Henry crouched down for protection from the blast. He knew it would have been too late to save him, but he did it anyway. Two more explosions in the same area kicked up dust and debris. The concussive force of the blasts shook the tower.

"MORTARS!" shouted Heart as he sprinted to the vehicle for cover.

"Doc, hand me that ammo!" Henry shouted.

"Here!" Taylor said, passing the ammo up "I'm going to check on the other guys."

Henry loaded the ammo into the machine gun and began to return fire. The sounds of cracking all around him grew louder as the insurgents focused their fire on him. One insurgent emerged from the trees to fire. Henry picked him off with an extended burst of the machine gun. The man just dropped to the ground, but nothing like in the movies. Henry expected him to flail about clutching his chest, but instead, he just dropped.

Between bursts of fire, Henry could hear some screams coming from behind him. Sounds like Fields… The Doc's got it, he thought to himself. He needed to focus on his job. The sounds of the mortars had stopped now, and he could hear Tremblay cheering in triumph for taking out the mortar crew. He glanced over to see Tremblay pumping a fist in the air through the smoke and dust. The sounds of gunfire from the marijuana field started to die down as the enemy combatants were overwhelmed by fire superiority. Suddenly, a massive force knocked

Henry on his ass. He went to stand back up and that's when the pain hit him. It felt like a million needles all stabbing him in the same spot in the chest. He coughed, and blood spit up into the air, raining back down on his face. As everything started to get dark, he could faintly see Sergeant Howard coming up the tower stairs. He knelt down next to Henry.

"MEDIC!" he yelled as he started to tear Henry's body armor off. He applied pressure to the bullet hole in Henry's chest, but the blood was escaping to fast. It began making its way to the tower floor, staining the plywood boards. "It's okay kid…. you're gunna be okay."

A BETTER PLAN

Khalid Almasi stood in line staring straight forward. His eyes slowly scanning the airport for security staff. His palms were sweaty. He hadn't been this nervous since his first firefight against the Americans in Iraq nearly twelve years ago. He was just a teenager then. The fighting had not reached his village yet, but you could hear the distant explosions in nearby Baghdad. The constant sound of fighter jets screaming overhead, followed by a distant boom. He would tell his family he was leaving for work in the fields but would drive to Baghdad to fight.

The airport loud speaker squawked something about loading zones snapping him back from his thoughts. Khalid moved forward with the line, sliding his carry-on bag with his foot. His handler had instructed him to dress to blend in, in order to minimize suspicions. Before he departed Libya, he was given a brand-new navy-blue suit with brown buttons, a white dress shirt, brown leather oxford shoes and a pink heather tie. He had stood there with the suit in his hands taking in the fabric. Inside the jacket pocket was a fake passport and a one-way plane ticket to Boston.

The line moved forward again. The couple ahead of Khalid grumbled about the time it takes to get through customs. The busy airport hummed with sounds of people chatting and muffled airliners taking off. The couple finally moved up to the customs desk a few moments later. He took a deep breath. He was next. Another few minutes passed, and the customs officer waved for Khalid to come forward. He picked up his bag and moved up against the desk, placing his passport and ticket on the counter for the officer. The customs officer grabbed the documents and asked whether he was there for business or pleasure. Khalid paused and took a quick breath. "Umm, business," he said. The officer flipped through the passport for a few more seconds and then proceeded to ask if Khalid had anything to declare. Khalid's hands were shaking slightly. He placed his left hand into his pants pocket. "All I have is my clothes," Khalid managed to get out. SLAM! The officer stamped the passport. Khalid jumped a little. The force of the stamp shocked him. The customs officer wished him a good stay and waved for the next traveler to come up. Khalid grabbed his bag and made his way to the taxi stand as he breathed a sigh of relief.

***

May 19th, 2010
Boston, Massachusetts

Khalid spent a day and a half exploring Boston. He took in the sights and sound of the city, including a tour of Harvard University. A man from Ireland scheduled a meeting with Khalid at 10am to assess his role in a planned attack, so before he grabbed a taxi he stopped at a nearby café and grabbed a coffee. He watched the people walk by on the street as he stood there sipping his drink. Very few people acknowledged him. Most were on their way to a baseball game nearby; others were heading to nearby restaurants for dinner. He climbed into a taxi that was waiting outside of the café and instructed the driver to take him to a warehouse in East Boston near the airport. The taxi arrived at the warehouse twenty-five minutes later. Khalid tipped the driver generously and stepped out of the taxi. The warehouse district was a stark difference from the bustling old buildings of downtown.

Inside the warehouse, large crates scattered the floor, surrounded by men armed with sub-machine guns. Along the catwalks were a few men armed with rifles. They patrolled the length of the building, looking outward towards the streets. A forklift beeped as it reversed from a shipping container carrying another large crate. The beeping echoed throughout the building. One of the men on the catwalk shouted something down to the group on the floor. The group of men made their way to a shipping bay door where a truck was backing into the loading dock. Khalid waited for the truck to finish backing and then made his way through a large brown windowless door next to the shipping bay. A man in a black leather jacket and brown cargo pants approached him, firming up his grip on his Vector 9mm SMG. He asked Khalid for his passport. Khalid's palms began to sweat. Another bead of sweat ran from his brow. He handed his passport to the man who flipped it open to the picture. He glanced back and forth from the picture to Khalid. "Any problems getting in?" he asked. His voice was gruff with a thick Irish accent. Khalid shook his head no. The man closed the passport and tucked it into the inside pocket of his leather jacket. He relaxed his grip on his sub-machine gun, lowering it to his side. "I'm O'Malley," he said. "Suits are meeting in the office upstairs. If ya need anything come find me." Khalid nodded and picked up his travel bag. He made his way to the stairs leading to the catwalk. O'Malley continued over to the truck and began to direct the unloading of more crates similar to the ones on the warehouse floor.

***

Khalid stood against the back wall of the large office; his hands in his pockets. Ten people sat around a large table in the centre, another ten standing with Khalid. Everyone was wearing the same blue suit with brown buttons, white shirt and pink heather tie. Khalid unbuttoned his suit jacket and straightened out his tie. The office door whipped open and O'Malley walked in and moved to the left, standing out of the way of the door. Everyone adjusted themselves in their seats. Khalid stepped away from the wall and straightened his posture. A few of the people cleared their throats. Another man walked into the room and stopped at the head of the table. He turned to face the crowd and leaned forward placing both his fists on the table. His beard was fire red and his face was pale with a scar on his left cheek extending up past his eye. The room was completely silent now. The only noise was the faint beeping of the forklift reversing down on the warehouse floor. "I'm Braden Murphy," the man said. He stood back up and crossed his arms across his chest. "You're here because you have been selected by your organizations as martyrs," he continued, "Martyrs to bring the world to justice. To bring it to order. To take it back from those who oppose

God and seek to line their pockets!" Khalid and the rest of the room were nodding in agreement. He heard a few exclamations of 'Fuck Yes!' and 'Allahu Akbar!'.

By now, Braden was pacing back and forth at the front of the room. Khalid could see his holstered pistol clearly now. Literally everyone is armed, he thought to himself. Another man entered briefly and passed a briefcase to O'Malley. O'Malley placed it onto the table while Braden continued to speak about bringing the world to justice. His voice growing louder and louder after each pause. O'Malley opened the briefcase. "We will now assign you your cities," Braden said, resting his right hand on his pistol. "Once you have your city, leave and head down to the warehouse floor and you'll be assigned a crate and transport truck to your destination," He said calmly. Khalid took a deep breath. One of the men around the table scoffed at the plan. He suggested that if he were in charge he would not use martyrs. He looked around the table at the other martyrs faces only to realize none of them shared his thoughts. Braden drew his pistol, a brand-new FN Five-Seven with a black slide and tan body and pointed it at the man. He pulled the trigger. Khalid jumped at the sound of the shot as it filled the room. He glanced over at the outspoken man and cringed at the sight of blood and brains splattered on the wall. The room then fell silent. "You're here for one reason and one alone," Braden said, holstering his pistol.

O'Malley continued to read out names and cities. After each name was read a martyr would get up and leave. Five minutes later, only O'Malley, Braden and Khalid stood in the room. O'Malley closed the briefcase and made his way back to the warehouse floor. Braden motioned for Khalid to come closer. Khalid nodded and made his way across the room. "I've got something special in mind for you," He said. "I've heard about your victories in Iraq against the Americans and I think it would be a shame to waste a man of your talents in an explosion." Braden paused briefly and then moved over to the desk behind him. He pulled down an old roll up world map hanging on the wall behind the desk. On it were cities coloured red and a few with green circles. He pointed to one inside a green circle. "Ever been to Pittsburgh?" He formed a smile through his beard.

.

FOG OF WAR

August 21st, 2020

Reading Pennsylvania

"The fog is heavy today," Henry Carson said, his mouth covered by his scarf. He kept watch through a cracked basement window while Jonathan Tremblay packed his day bag.

"Yeah, I don't like it," Tremblay replied, while shoving his ranger blanket into his bag.

"How are we doing for ammo?" Henry asked. His gaze still laser focused on the outside. Tremblay looked at the Light Machine Gun on the table next to Henry.

"I've got one box of five five six in my bag plus the box on the LMG… You?" he said, worriedly.

"Shit, I've only got four mags left," Henry replied. His voice wavering with a slight worried tone.

Tremblay tightened the straps on his bag and tucked them up under the top flap, so they weren't dangling. He put the pack on, securing the chest strap. He was a perfectionist. Everything had to be neat and tidy and squared away. As Tremblay walked over to the window where Henry was standing, he grabbed Henry's SCAR-L rifle which was leaning against the wall. The rifle appeared well used, with some of the tan paint chipping off and some dirt around the ACOG sight. Tremblay tapped Henry's leg with the side of the barrel. "Shouldn't be that far from you," he said. Henry grinned and reminded Tremblay of the time he had left his LMG on his bed when they came under Taliban fire in Afghanistan. Tremblay brushed it off, only showing a slight smirk. "When are we heading back to base?" Tremblay asked, changing the subject abruptly.

"As soon as Brynn and Ahmed get back…" Henry began to reply.

POK POK POK! The sounds of AK-47 fire, muffled by the fog and surrounding houses, rang out across the barren subdivision.

"FUCK!" Tremblay shouted as he shoved Henry out of the way. He grabbed his LMG, swung the basement window open and raised the weapon up, placing the bipod just outside on the grass. He was gazing hard as though he could see for miles. POK POK POK POK POK! Another AK-47 sounds off. More rounds this time, much less controlled and more panicked sounding.

Henry ran over and unlocked the basement door, then headed over to the other window with his rifle, peering through his sight, looking for any signs of movement. The clicking sound of Tremblay flipping his weapons safety off echoed through the quiet basement. "Easy…" Henry said. "Identify friend or foe". Through the silence and controlled breathing, the sounds of footsteps thudding across grass made their way through the fog. Someone was sprinting towards the basement window. The sounds of the footsteps grew louder and began to sound like a stampede of cattle.

"SIERRA TANGO! SIERRA TANGO!" a female voice screamed

through the fog.

Sierra Tango... the running password Henry had given Brynn and Ahmed before they set out on their recon around the neighbourhood. It allowed them to identify someone running towards them as friends. It was the first two letters of the word STEAK, Tremblay's favourite food. Shortly after shouting the password, Brynn emerged through the thick fog, sprinted up the front steps to the house and crashed through the front door.

"One," Tremblay whispered to himself, counting his teammate. More footsteps thudded their way across the grass. This time they sounded heavier.

"SEATTLE TANGO! SEATTLE TANGO!" a man's voice shouted through the fog. Tremblay moved his finger overtop of the trigger, took aim, and slowly began to squeeze.

"Wait!" Henry said in a loud whisper, motioning with his left hand slow down. Just then, Ahmed appeared from the fog in full sprint. Ahmed Elamin was originally from Pakistan, and sometimes had troubles pronouncing words in English. He jumped up the front steps and dove through the front door behind Brynn, kicking it shut.

"Jesus..." Tremblay exclaimed. "That's two," he said as he took a deep breath. His heart was nearly in his throat now. The sounds of more footsteps moving towards the house were getting louder. They thudded on the dewy grass in rapid succession.

"Get ready," Henry said, firming his grip on his rifle. Tremblay squeezed the trigger on his machine gun. The sound of the gun firing echoed through the basement, causing Henry to cringe and devastated their eardrums as Tremblay let loose a massive twenty round burst.

The rounds tore through the man shaped figure that emerged from the fog. He dropped with a final thud, his momentum causing him to slide another foot or so. Just then, Brynn and Ahmed came in through the basement door, breathing heavy, Brynn clutching her upper left arm.

"It's… an NBF… patrol," she said bent over and between breaths. Ahmed immediately began to grab a bandage and wrap it around Brynn's arm. "Only four of them," she said through clenched teeth as Ahmed tightened the bandage.

"Three now," Tremblay replied, maintaining watch.

"We better move, out through the back, into the woods," Henry replied, grabbing his day bag. "You okay Brynn?" he asked motioning to her wound.

"I'm fine…" she replied through the pain.

"It's a graze, but it will need to be cleaned and stitched," Ahmed interjected.

"I'm fine!"

"Alright, once we get to the rendezvous point, we will send up a SIT-REP and head back to the base. Got it? Let's move!" Henry commanded.

Ahmed set out first, scanning the fog before stepping out the back door. Henry watched as Ahmed had gone about five feet and disappeared into the thick whitish-grey vapor. He stepped out and motioned for Brynn and Tremblay to follow him. They made their way across the back yards in the subdivision, making use of the broken fences and the concealment offered up by the fog.

They were well informed of the NBF, but had never encountered them before, until this patrol. The New Boston Front was a rapidly expanding radical group that had only recently established a foothold in Pennsylvania. Their leader has a brutality about him that has led to soldiers deserting the group in search for a better life. Even the Federation has some former NBF fighters in its ranks. Command informed Henry and his team, before they set out on patrol to Reading, that this radical group operates in four-man detachments but never far from support. Their objective was to see how close to base this group was getting and to observe their troop strength and movements. We have to move fast! Henry thought. As they disappeared into the tree line, they could hear faint muffled yelling from behind them.

"Sounds like they found their buddy," Tremblay whispered.

They picked up the pace and made it to the rendezvous point a few minutes later. After Henry counted the team, they sat quietly in place. They just listened. There was the faint sound of birds chirping, but that was all. At least we aren't being followed, Henry thought. After an uneventful five minutes had passed, Henry pressed the switch on his radio to send a situation report.

"One this is One Four Delta, SITREP, over," Henry whispered into the mic.

"One send," the radio operator replied.

"One Four Delta, Enemy: four times fighting age males at grid 1473 – 6090, one KIA," He paused and took a deep breath. "Friendly: At grid 1444 – 6066, engaged enemy, one wounded. Heading back, over."

"One, roger, out," the radio operator signed off.

Brynn let out a small groan, grasping her bullet wound. Time to move, thought Henry. He tapped Ahmed on the shoulder and motioned to keep traveling west. As they stood up, he tapped Tremblay's boot to signal that they were moving. Tremblay stood up, collapsed his LMG's bipod and followed the team.

***

After an hour of slow walking through the woods, the fog had lifted. It was close to ten o'clock and the sky was clear for a late August morning. It was quiet too. The chirping birds had grown a little louder now, but not by much. Henry started to think about how this area used to be full of people walking their dogs, or hiking and now… now, it was just a war zone. As he continued to think about the past, Ahmed stopped in his tracks. Henry was in a daze and almost walked right into him. Ahmed motioned to the front, and then Henry saw the truck. A pickup truck in decent shape, just passed the tree line. "Could be a trap," Ahmed said with hesitation in his voice.

"Only one way to find out," Tremblay replied, passing his LMG to Ahmed. "Give me your AK."

Henry motioned to Brynn to watch the rear, as he and Ahmed moved a few feet forward to provide cover for Tremblay. Tremblay moved towards the truck slowly, taking his time, and stepping carefully. He kept his eyes out for trip wires, or wires that could detonate an Improvised Explosive Device. He had learned a valuable lesson in Afghanistan. Never get complacent. On almost every patrol, Tremblay was always up front with his LMG, while Henry was behind him navigating. One day, during a patrol into village they had visited hundreds of times, he almost stepped on a trip wire hooked up to an anti-tank mine paired with sixty liters of homemade explosive. Henry had spotted it at the last second and screamed into his personal radio for Tremblay to stop moving. Nei-

33

ther of them ever forgot that day.

As Tremblay approached the passenger side of the truck, he took a quick look underneath and at each tire. They all seemed to be good, he thought to himself, nothing to go boom. He peered inside through the passenger window and saw an MP-5 9mm submachine gun, and more importantly, the keys! "Shit," he whispered to himself. Whoever owns this truck is close or stupid, he thought. He pulled his glove back, exposing his wrist and quietly pressed it against the hood. Warm! He's close and stupid! He looked back at the team and signaled them to hurry. The team quickly reached him and huddled up, Ahmed facing the way they came.

"SITREP," he said. "There's an MP-5 in the cab with the keys, and the engine is warm".

"Good, get the fuck in the driver's seat through this side, Brynn and Ahmed, in the bed with the LMG, quietly…. GO!" Henry replied.

As Tremblay climbed into the cab, he passed the MP-5 out to Brynn, who grinned with excitement. Ahmed quietly moved to the back and lowered the tailgate. He helped Brynn in, and passed her the LMG so he could climb in. Henry quietly placed the team's day bags into the truck bed over the side. As Henry was climbing into the cab, Brynn quietly tapped on the rear window. "Two guys in the south-west tree line," she said, pointing to them.

"Punch it Trembles!" Henry shouted. The truck engine roared to life as Tremblay turned the key and stepped on the gas. A voice began to shout from the trees. The two men scrambled to ready their weapons and fire on the car thieves. CRACK! CRACK! CRACK! The sound of bullets breaking the sound barrier as they missed their target and whizzed past the truck. One round slammed into the tail light, causing Brynn to flinch.

"CONTACT!" Brynn screamed. She let loose three short bursts from the MP-5 in return, causing the men to duck for cover.

"One this is One Four Delta, Contact, wait out!" Henry screamed into his radio microphone. Ahmed scrambled to the back of the truck to close the tailgate as the truck sped away.

"GET DOWN!" Ahmed shouted in terror. The tree line ignited with a thick puff of white smoke and a flash of flame. A deep whoosh mixed with a higher pitched scream attacked their ear drums as a rocket propelled grenade tore through the air, narrowly missing the truck, and detonating a few feet in front of it. The explosion sent dirt, debris, and smoke through the air coupled with a thudding vibration that worked its way through the truck. It was an uneasy feeling that Henry would never get used to. The kind of feeling that made your bones ache and stomach turn. As the truck emerged through the smoke, Tremblay could make out a road to the North. He wrenched on the steering wheel and the truck darted in that direction. He weaved through a hailstorm of bullets like a football player juking a defensive line. Behind them, the sounds of machine gun fire rang out and echoed off the surrounding trees. Ahmed had gotten back up and was suppressing the area where the RPG came from. He was pressed firmly against the tailgate, hoping it wouldn't open and send him tumbling out of the truck.

The black off-road tires screeched a banshee like shriek as soon as the truck contacted the faded and cracked pavement. Henry pressed the talk switch on his radio and called in a contact report. "One this is One Four Delta, contact at grid 1375 – 5933. Two times fighting age males with small arms. We are suppressing as we withdraw. Time, now, over," Henry said into the microphone.

"One, roger, out," the radio operator replied.

"How are we doing for gas?" Henry asked Tremblay.

"Half a tank," Tremblay replied, checking his mirrors.

"Good, we'll make it," Henry breathed a sigh of relief.

***

It had been a half an hour of driving since they engaged the RPG team in the woods, and everyone was exhausted. Brynn was fast asleep in the truck bed, buried in a pile of backpacks, while Ahmed maintained watch to the rear. Tremblay looked as though he was out for a Sunday drive through the countryside. He was calm and collected; he even signaled his turns like the old days. Henry was a little more shaken up. It was definitely not the first time someone shot at him. In fact, he was fine with combat. Nevertheless, this was his first command.

Their objective had been to scout the area around Reading and confirm reports that NBF troops were venturing into new territories. On the first day of their patrol, a group of civilians compromised their position and alerted a nearby NBF team. Henry set up to ambush them, and a lucky stray round struck the NBF radio. With no way to call for backup, Henry and the team were able to eliminate the threat. He thought about how the second and third days were much better. They were able to observe enemy movement uncompromised. They weren't so lucky on the last morning of their operation, and to top it off, he had a wounded soldier. I guess we did accomplish the mission, he thought to himself. He pulled out his map and marked the contact locations on them to report to command.

"We'll be there in thirty," Tremblay said. "Get some rack".

"Yeah, I might. Gotta be fresh looking when I get to HQ."

DEBRIEF. ORDERS. GEAR UP.

The New Cumberland Army Depot in Harrisburg Pennsylvania is the last standing military base in the Eastern United States. It is now the home to thirty thousand soldiers and a small force of helicopters. The fighting units in Harrisburg largely consisted of the Tenth Mountain Division, the Twenty-Eighth Infantry Division, the Second Canadian Division and a small Special Forces unit called SOFREC. The military units of the Federation of North America operated under one joint command headed by a tribunal consisting of Pedro St.Marco the President of Mexico, François Lafontaine the Prime Minister of Canada, and Stephanie Lawson the President of the United States.

Towards the end of 2010 when most of the world was recovering from an Economic Recession; a radical group known as the Republic Sabres carried out a coordinated attack on countries around the globe. The late November attacks decimated most major cities, military infrastructure, and resources across the world. North America and Europe were hit the hardest and as they fell, more groups rose to join the Republic cause. These groups were all lead by individuals who operated as War Lords, claiming territory like gangs, with members loyal only to them. Slowly, over the following years the individual groups collapsed to infighting and conflicts between them. Now, only three major factions remained in North America. The New Boston Front, the Republic Sabres and the Western Mountain Alliance.

***

Tremblay eased the truck to a stop outside of the SOFREC tent lines. His face gleamed with delight, like a child with a new toy at Christmas. He had big plans to modify his new toy.

"Nice Ride!" a voice shouted from a short distance away.

"Thanks Colonel," Henry replied, stepping down from the tall truck cab. He turned to look at Colonel Howard who was walking towards them, wearing a stoic look on his face. Colonel James Howard, a man in his forties, is a younger man for his rank, but being a brilliant strategist made him an effective leader. He had a special rapport with Captain Henry Carson and Lieutenant Jonathan Tremblay; he was their section commander in Afghanistan back when he was a Sergeant.

"We jacked it off some asshole who went for a piss!" Tremblay chimed in.

"Ha! Good on ya!"

Colonel Howard slapped Brynn on the back, forcing a lengthy groan from her body. She clutched her wounded arm. Henry motioned with his head for Brynn to leave and have her arm tended to at the Medical tent. Ahmed followed her, carrying her gear.

"Get your kit squared away, then meet me at HQ when you're ready Captain."

"Sir," Henry replied.

39

Henry and Tremblay unloaded the weapons and bags from the truck and carried them into the tent. The weight of the bags pulled on their tired arms. They placed the bags on the corresponding bed spaces and locked Brynn's rifle and her new MP-5 in the weapons locker. Tremblay smiled at the guns and pulled a cigar out of his breast pocket. He lit it up in a quick flash of flame and smoke from a match and followed Henry to the HQ building to meet Colonel Howard.

"I'm gunna stop at the armory," Tremblay said as he started walking away from Henry. Henry gave him a quick wave and told him he would brief the team as a whole later.

***

Ahmed helped Brynn up onto the medics table and began to un-wrap the bandage he had applied to her arm earlier. By now, blood had seeped through the bandage and the pain was as intense as ever. Ahmed was a doctor in Pakistan and served as the teams' medic, so Brynn was more than comfortable with his abilities. She winced as the last bit of gauze pulled at the open wound. The skin pulled, then snapped back like a hair being plucked. Once the bandage was off, Ahmed assessed the damage. The blood ran down her arm like a thick water.

"It's not too deep."

"It's stupid."

"Shit happens, and it's impressive you made it this long without taking a round."

He motioned with his head downward. Brynn followed his head downward towards his thigh.

"Oh… Right," she said, remembering last summer when he took a 9mm round to the leg, "That was quite the day, huh."

"Yeah, like something out of a movie," he chuckled. Brynn took her hand and turned his head so he was looking directly in her wide brown eyes. Her auburn hair coming out of the messy bun at the back of her head.

"Hey…" she said pausing to choke back a tear, "Thanks for saving me back there." She leaned in and pressed her lips to his, shortly forgetting the pain in her arm.

"Not a problem!" he replied matter-of-factly. "Besides, Tremblay would kill me if I lost the team eye candy!" She lightly pushed his face back towards her wound, biting her lip as he started to stitch her up.

***

August 29th, 2020
Harrisburg, Pennsylvania

Tremblay grunted as he lifted the fifty-caliber machine gun barrel and inserted it into the gun, locking it into place. He dusted off his pants and used his forearm to wipe the sweat away from his forehead. He jumped down from the back of the pickup truck and took a few paces back to admire his work. He wiped his hands off on his tan t-shirt and pulled a cigar from his cargo pocket. He placed it between his teeth, biting down ever so slightly.

"Lookin' good Trembles!" Henry said walking up behind him.

"That ought-a help us kill some fuckers," He replied. "I'll go do that ammo run now".

"Sure thing. I'll brief the team after we get some rest."

Brynn was relaxing on her cot, reading an old book she always carried with her. Her arm, perfectly bandaged by Ahmed, and propped on a pillow for support. Her hair tucked neatly behind her head. Before the war, Brynn Parker was a corporate lawyer from New York City. She used to work the hardest in her firm, dreaming of making partner and when she was not nose deep in work, she would read. She loved to read Harry Potter; it was her favourite book series. She loved to get lost in the fantasy world of magic and wizards. She never admitted this fact though as her work friends would never have let her live that down. A tear began to roll down her face as she thought about her old life. She used the photo of her old dog; a black Maltese named Aurora, to mark her page before she dropped the book and covered her face to hide her tears. As she cried, she thought about the day the attacks began. The day her world ended. She had to meet a client in Pittsburgh to go over a new shareholder agreement for his company. She decided to take a couple extra days and drive there, so she could stop in Harrisburg Pennsylvania to visit her parents. As she drove into downtown Harrisburg, she started to notice that there was hardly any traffic. She flipped the radio on, nothing but static. When she pulled into her parents' driveway and got out of the car, her mother came running down the front steps in tears and threw herself onto Brynn. After wiping her tears away, Brynn's mother began to tell her what had happened. In the largest coordinated terrorist attack in the world's history, members of a radical group known as the Republic Sabres had successfully detonated mass destruction devices in major cities and military bases across the world. Radical forces spared some cities from destruction and took them over by force.

Brynn broke down as she realized that New York was among the list of destroyed cities.

She moved her book off her chest and began to wipe her tears away with her scarf. Henry began to sit up after a well-deserved rest. As he sat up on his cot, he noticed Brynn was crying.

"You ok?"

"Yeah, it's just… you know, it doesn't get easier, thinking about what happened," Brynn replied.

"Yeah, I know. That's why we fight," Henry said, rubbing his eyes. As he stood up and reached for his shirt, Brynn could see a scar on his chest.

"What's that from?" she asked.

"Oh, took a round in Afghanistan back in Oh Eight," He replied, looking down at his scar rubbing it with his fingers.

"Now we match," she said smiling and pointing to her bandaged arm. Henry smiled and continued to put on his shirt. He looked around but couldn't see Tremblay or Ahmed anywhere.

"Where are those clowns?"

"Tremblay is showing Ahmed the new truck," she replied. Henry headed over to the door, stopping at the doorway.

"You sure you're ok?" he said over his shoulder.

"Hells yes!" Brynn said with enthusiasm. "I'm ready to kick some ass!"

"Good," Henry replied. "We are heading out soon."

He headed out to the truck to grab Tremblay and Ahmed. They were both smoking cigars and admiring the new modifications to the truck. What was once a somewhat nice black Ford F-250 was now an armored reconnaissance vehicle for the team. Tremblay had installed a fifty-caliber machine gun in the bed and added some steel plating around the truck to provide extra protection. "She's a little fatter now, but the V8 will get the job done," Tremblay said as Henry walked over to them. A smirk formed on Henry's face. He slapped Tremblay on the back and motioned for them to head towards the tent. The three of them turned and headed back into the tent for their briefing, Tremblay locking the doors to the truck with the key fob.

With a map of the area laid out on the floor, Henry used a collapsible pointer, like an antenna from the controller of a remote controlled car, to point to locations on the map. "Our objective is to meet up with Four Two armored recce platoon," Henry started. "And to provide security for their road move back here."

"What a bunch of pussies," Tremblay chuckled.

"Agreed, but they ran into some resistance and are down a vehicle and have 6 vital signs absent," Henry replied sternly. He raised his eyes from the map to assess the teams' reactions. They were all as he had expected. Pale and vacant, like they had seen a ghost.

"Shit," Brynn gasped.

"What were they up to Cap?" Ahmed asked.

"Their mission was to scout north of Pittsburgh in an area called Butler. HQ is looking at using it as a staging area for an assault on the city."

Henry used the pointer to draw attention to the location of Butler. Henry briefly explained the plan to the team, noting that they will travel half way, leaving just before sundown, and continue the following day at the same time. He asked to Tremblay to take the new truck to the vehicle depot so they can deactivate the daytime running lights and so they can install infrared lights for driving by night vision goggles.

"What's the route?" Tremblay asked.

"I was thinking we should take the I-76 West, then head north to Johnstown and set up a camp on the outskirts," Henry replied. He pointed Johnstown with his collapsible pointer, drawing a circle around it.

"Safe bet," Tremblay said, "We have a small out-post there if we need support."

"Alright," Henry said, clearing his throat. "Order of March: Trembles you're driving. I'm shotgun. Ahmed on the fifty. And Brynn, rear security. We'll switch up as needed." Everyone nodded in agreement. Ahmed folded up the map and grabbed his note pad and pens while Tremblay headed for the door.

"Oh," Henry said while putting his notepad away, "Fighting gear only. Let's keep it heavy on the guns, light on the crap."

Brynn chuckled as she started to clean her newly acquired MP-5.

"And get some rest, we leave at nightfall."

REUNION

I-76 was once a busy Interstate highway filled with commuters, travelers, family and friends. Now it is an empty over grown extremely long stretch of road. When the first attacks happened, and people started to flee the cities, the military closed all of the highways to use as emergency landing strips for the Air Force. Henry thought back to the first day of attacks, back home in Canada nearly ten years ago. He was on his way home to Toronto after his first completed semester in University. All he could think about was how proud he was of himself for going back to school and being the only combat experienced person in his class. As he gazed through the truck windows at the empty I-76, he remembered the busy highway he was driving along when his car radio cut out on him. As he scanned for other working radio stations, he noticed traffic had begun to slow down. It was almost crawling. As traffic came to a dead stop, he managed to find a faded local station from a nearby town. Henry stayed in his car, a deep blue Subaru Impreza, and listened to the broadcast while other travelers got out and asked each other what was going on. The news was devastating. Toronto, Vancouver, New York, Los Angeles, Houston, Paris, and Rome. The list went on. Almost all cities had been destroyed. The memories assaulted him like soldiers storming a castle.

"We're rolling up on Johnstown in fifteen," Tremblay said, jolting back Henry from his thoughts.

"Good, cut the pace," Henry said as he leaned back to open the cab's rear window. "Ahmed, we'll be in view of Johnstown in fifteen, crack the I-R glow stick in the radio antenna and keep your eyes peeled, pass it on."

Ahmed stood up from the bed of the truck to crack the glow stick; the muffled sounds of his words to Brynn, heard slightly over the sounds of the truck. Henry began to examine the map for their location, getting ready to direct Tremblay into the bushes for cover. "OP Johnstown this is One Four Delta," Henry said into his radio.

"OP Johnstown send, over," a tired sounding voice replied.

"One Four Delta roger, we are approaching from the south via route two one niner, please advise on possible enemy presence, over."

"OP Johnstown. Ugh..." the sleep deprived voice stalled. "Ugh, roger, we have had sporadic attacks on patrols over the last two weeks. Ugh, yeah... over".

Henry sighed, lowered the radio handset and looked over at Tremblay. "What do you think?" he asked.

"You know me Henry, I'm a rugged outdoorsman, but I'm not one to pass up a free bed, and a chance to see Brynn in the shower," Tremblay said, producing a perverted grin. Henry smacked Tremblay on the shoulder. As much as he loved Johnathan, he hated how he treated women like objects.

"OP Johnstown, this is One Four Delta, requesting permission to crash your party, over," Henry said into the handset, smiling.

"Ugh, sure…shit, I mean, OP Johnstown, Roger, out!" the radio operator fumbled. Henry radioed back to Colonel Howard at HQ and informed him of the change of plan. The Colonel agreed to and suggested they steal some supplies while they are there. Steal what you can from wherever you go, Henry thought to himself. Howard used to say that to his soldiers whenever they entered a new friendly camp back in Afghanistan. Those were the days.

The truck rolled to a stop outside of a dimly lit tent in the centre of the outpost. Light flickered through small holes in the tent as soldiers inside walked by the dimly lit lanterns. Tremblay took note of the height, location and spread of the holes. Probably bullets, but might be airburst mortars, he thought to himself. The frightening thing about airburst was that if you didn't have a good solid roof over your head, you didn't stand a chance. Fighting back a yawn, Henry opened the door and made his way to the tent with his rifle. It had been a long night of driving and he was looking forward to some sleep. As Henry disappeared into the tent, Ahmed jumped down from the back of the truck.

"Where's he going?" he asked Brynn.

"Probably just to check in with the outpost commander," she replied.

"I hope he's not long. I would like to be asleep before the sun starts to rise," he said grumpily while removing his tactical vest.

Henry emerged from the tent a few moments later, letting out another yawn. "Third tent on the left is ours for the day," He said motioning with his rifle. Tremblay shifted the truck into gear and slowly made his way to the tent, leaving Ahmed and Henry to walk the fifty-or-so metres.

***

"Hey Carson!" Brynn shouted from the passenger seat of the truck cab.

"Yeah?" Henry shouted down from the fifty-cal.

"I forgot to show you what I stole from Johnstown!" she replied, "Ahmed, move that green tarp."

"Holy shit!" Ahmed shouted. Henry glanced down to see four M-72 Light Anti-Tank rockets. The biggest grin began to spread across Henry's face, as if he was kid at Christmas again. "Well. Fucking. Done." He said to himself in a whispered voice.

Tremblay shouted in excitement, "I knew I loved you." Brynn smiled and shoved Tremblay's shoulder.

As the truck began to crest a hill, Tremblay began to slow down and pulled off the road to the right. He moved the truck into a tree line for concealment and shut the engine off. "It should be day light in an hour, so I'll take first watch while you three eat and piss," he said. Henry nodded to Ahmed who dropped the tailgate of the truck and began digging into some rations. Brynn wandered off behind a tree while Tremblay set up his LMG in the bushes to watch down the road.

***

The recently up-armored pickup they commandeered seemed to be handling quite well, even with the extra weight of steel plates and a machine gun. Henry noticed a couple of bumps that caused the tires to rub in the wheel wells but assumed that Tremblay already has plans to correct that. We should be getting close to Four Two, He thought to himself; now back in the cab operating the radio. He preferred the passenger seat over the machine gun anyway. An uneasy feeling started to creep up on him at the thought of how uneventful the trip had been. He remembered the briefing he got from Colonel Howard before they left. He had told him that there had been a moderate to heavy presence of patrols from Pittsburgh, usually small teams of six, but there had been reports of thirty to forty-person patrols. Platoon size…. Shit… Henry thought. Pittsburgh was the first North American city captured by the Sabres. After years of resistance, it finally fell to the Republic. Pittsburgh is now under the command of General Almasi and his Sabre forces. The Colonel had told Henry that what the Sabres lack in tech, they more than make up for in brutality. "Four Two this One Four Delta, Over," Henry said calmly into the radio mic.

"Four Two Send," a voice whispered back.

"One Four, roger, we are approximately two klicks from your position moving along route four-two-two now, over," Henry replied in the most professional voice he could muster.

"Four Two, roger, recommend you move along the train tracks to our position, this place crawls," the voice whispered back.

"One Four Roger, sit tight, out," Henry ended the conversation.

After directing Tremblay onto the train tracks, he began to scan the buildings on the right of the truck. He rolled down the window and propped the body of his SCAR-L on the doorframe for support. Ahmed was scanning forward and left into the trees with the fifty-cal., while Brynn laid in the bed of the truck with Tremblay's LMG propped up on the tailgate for rear security. We got this… Henry thought to himself as he tried to control his breathing. The sun was just beginning to rise behind them, casting a warm glow over the buildings to their front. "Four Two this is One Four Delta, approximately ONE klick from your position, please don't shoot us!" Henry said nervously into the mic.

"Why aren't they saying anything?" Tremblay asked. His voice was noticeably shaky

Ahmed shouted. "CONTACT FRONT!" He swung the fifty-caliber machine gun towards a roof top about five hundred metres in front of them. He squeezed the trigger. It was too late. The figure on the roof fired an RPG towards the direction of Four Two, seconds before Ahmed's volley cut him down. The brass fifty-caliber casings falling onto the trucks roof sounded like a strange metallic rain. A faint distant boom echoed over the deafening blasts from the machine gun above their heads. As they picked up speed to move closer, gunshots rang out from a warehouse yard on the right.

"Tremblay, push left into the trees, we'll ditch the truck and move in on foot," Henry commanded. The truck crashed through some bushes as it came to a halt, kicking up dead leaves and branches all around them. The truck slid to a halt and the team dismounted. "Four Two this is One Four Delta, moving to your location on foot from the east, do NOT engage us!" Henry yelled over the radio as they made their way to the closest warehouse building. The sounds of gunfire growing louder as they got closer.

Ahmed was the first to the building, a tall metal warehouse that looked like it no one had ever used it. He stacked up next to the closest door and waited for the team, breathing heavily and bouncing with a nervous energy. Tremblay was next up to the door. He pressed up behind Ahmed with such force, that it almost knocked him over. Henry was the next to fall in behind Tremblay, followed closely by Brynn. She reached forward and squeezed Henry's thigh. Henry reached forward, squeezing Tremblay's ass, as he always does when they breach a room. Smiling, Tremblay passed the squeeze forward to Ahmed. Here we go… Ahmed thought to himself. Without missing a beat, Ahmed spun into the open doorway, stepping in and turning to the left, all in one fluid motion. Like the body of a snake, the rest of the team followed Ahmed in. Tremblay turning to the right, Henry to the left, Brynn to the right.

"Left side clear," Ahmed said in a loud whisper.

"Right side clear," Tremblay reported.

"Door to the front," Brynn whispered.

"Seen," Henry acknowledged.

As the team made their way to the next door, Henry started picking apart their breach. Ahmed was a little hesitant on the initial breach, He thought. What are you doing!? This isn't the time!

"Movement in the next room," Brynn whispered, snapping Henry back from his thoughts. Brynn was the first up to the next door. With her newly acquired MP-5 she aimed at something in the next room. The others quickly and quietly moved in behind her. Ahmed sent the squeeze to move up from the back. Brynn was so laser focused, she didn't even realize Tremblay had squeezed her ass. Two men were standing in the centre of the room looking down at something on the floor, about fifty metres away. The Sabre's logo, a gold poorly painted sabre inside a red poorly painted circle on their backs like targets. TAK TAK TAK! Three suppressed 9mm rounds from Brynn's MP-5 flew across the room at subsonic speeds, ending their journey in the back of the man on the left, as Brynn moved into the room. She ducked behind some barrels for cover. In a state of confusion, the Sabre soldier on the right spun around. He raised his AK-47 with just enough time to see the barrel of Henry's SCAR-L pointed at him. BLAM! BLAM! The second Sabre soldier drops to the ground. The sounds of the gunfire echoed off the metal walls of the building.

"Tremblay, push forward and cover the front," Henry whispered loudly. "Ahmed, watch the rear, Brynn with me," he said motioning forward with his left hand. Henry and Brynn walked up to the two Sabre's they just dropped, hopping over stacks of steel beams scattered across the warehouse floor. Once they got closer, they were able to see what was so interesting to the two men.

"Shit, is he one of ours?" Brynn asked.

"Yeah, looks like a Mexican Officer," Henry replied. Henry knelt down over the officer and began to search him, while Brynn searched the two dead Sabre soldiers. Captain Garcia… shit. He was the CO of Four Two, Henry thought to himself as he read the deceased Captains nametag.

"Ugh…" Brynn said in disgust, "what happened to him?"

"Frag," Henry said, pointing to the shrapnel damage to the surrounding barrels and the Captains missing leg. The grenade had sent his leg across the room, lucky for him he was killed instantly. The gunfire from the other buildings had stopped now and things began to get eerily quiet. Outside, a vehicle engine started up. Then another. Henry motioned to the others to keep quiet. He firmed his grip on his rifle.

"I've got movement a head in the next room," Tremblay whispered.

As Tremblay tightened his grip around his machine gun, a voice called out from the other room.

"Carson? That you?" the voice said from the other room.

"Roger! Come out slowly," Henry replied. The voice appeared slowly in the darkened door as a bloodied William Heart, an M4 slung across his chest with his arms half way in the air.

"Fuck a duck!" Tremblay yelled standing up so fast he knocked over the barrels he was using for cover.

"Heart? Is that you?" Henry asked, surprised. Henry hadn't seen William Heart since a tour reunion barbeque in 2009 at Tremblay's house. He had not changed much, still had a baby face and non-regulation hair, which was noticeably greyer than before.

"Hey lovers!" Heart said, lowering his arms to embrace Tremblay's bear hug.

"We should head back to OP Johnstown before another patrol heads this way," Heart said.

"Agreed, I don't think I can handle any more man love," Brynn said.

"We'll help gather up your wounded and KIA and follow you out," Henry said slinging his rifle. Henry had not been this happy to see someone since he met up with Tremblay six months after the war began. He walked over and gave Heart a long bro-hug.

***

The mid-morning sun shinned bright in the cloudless sky. A few plumes of smoke from a couple of destroyed vehicles added a small haze to the air. Tremblay and Ahmed returned with the truck and assisted the rest of Four Two with the wounded. Henry and Heart were standing next to the destroyed command vehicle, partly catching up, partly discussing what happened. Heart explained that the command vehicle in their convoy hit a mine and the Sabres ambushed them when the troops dismounted to attempt a tire change. Henry stared at the vehicle. Smoke still rising from underneath. The jack and torque wrench laid next to the vehicle, covered in blood. As his gaze made its way upward, he made note of the bullet holes and marks in the armor. They were all from medium caliber weapons. Most likely 7.62 millimetre. "AK-47's?" Henry asked.

"Yeah, and fifty cal DShK," Heart replied, nodding upwards. Henry looked up at the turret for the Remote Weapon System. It looked like Swiss cheese. There were holes in the armor, and even two right through the body of the machine gun mounted in the turret. The belt of ammo hanging out of the box, swaying in the gentle morning breeze. Henry wafted some smoke away from his face.

"Alright, let's destroy the radio, weapons and any other working systems and move out," Henry said to Heart.

"We'll need some more C4, we only have one pound."

"It'll have to do," replied Henry. He made his way into the vehicle. The seats were soaked in blood and blood-stained bandages lined the floor. A helmet laid in the centre of the floor on top of the bandages, a hole through either side. Henry let out a slight gag as he opened the roof hatch and began to unhook the destroyed machine gun. Henry noticed the lack of spent casings on the roof. They didn't stand a chance, he thought to himself. He dropped the gun on the floor. Heart tossed a broken radio next to it.

"That's all there is," he said.

"Great," Henry replied. "We'll place the C4 and get to cover."

After they destroyed the equipment, the four-vehicle convoy headed east towards OP Johnstown. The black up-armored Ford looked out of place and miniature amongst the three, green reconnaissance LAV's. Heart stood up in the rear hatch of the second LAV. He made eye contact with Henry, who was riding shotgun in the pickup. He pointed at his own eyes, and then motioned upwards towards the buildings. The convoy took a sharp left turn. They were now entering a residential area with a number of small high-rise apartment buildings on both sides of the street. Henry rolled his window down and by the time he got his rifle propped up on the side mirror, Heart had already retreated into the LAV. A soldier with an LMG had replaced him. The soldier was visibly nervous. His body was trembling, and he was rapidly scanning the buildings for signs of movement. I don't blame him, Henry thought. It's been a rough few days. The convoy made a sudden sharp right turn. The soldier dropped back into the LAV. His foot slipping off the seat. As the pickup made the turn, Tremblay pointed out that the road appeared blocked on purpose. There were visible drag marks in the dirt on the road. Henry leaned back and slid open the rear window. "Eyes peeled," He said to Ahmed "somethings up."

The concussion from the blast was immense. Henry's breath pulled from his body as if he was in a vacuum. As he shook his head clear, he could hear Brynn swearing in the truck bed. The force of the blast had knocked her down. Muffled sounds of gunfire grew louder as Henry's hearing returned. THUNK THUNK THUNK! Three rounds slammed into the hood of the truck snapping Henry from his daze. He snapped his head to Tremblay who was already outside of the now stopped truck returning fire with Brynn's MP-5. The fifty-caliber sprung to life. The flame from the barrel was so bright Henry could see its reflection in the hood of the truck. As Henry exited the truck, debris from the explosion began raining down on them. A large black cloud was billowing from the front of the convoy. "FUCKING IED!" someone screamed.

Henry quickly took cover behind a burnt-out car next to Brynn. She was using Tremblay's LMG to suppress two men who were firing at the convoy from a high window on the left. Henry raised his rifle, taking aim at the window. Brynn ducked down behind the car to reload wiping sweat from her forehead with her wrist. As she did, a Sabre soldier with an AK-47 appeared in the window, rifle raised. BLAM! The soldier drops. Henry took a breath as he released the trigger of his rifle. He continued to slowly fire at the now empty window until Brynn finished reloading.

The fifty-caliber machine gun was deafening, roaring like a dragon as Ahmed suppressed the apartment building. He traversed his fire across the windows, then down to the street. He cut down two Sabres heading for cover behind a barricade. Ahmed shouted something to Henry, but he couldn't make it out over the sounds of the gunfire. The fifty-cal suddenly fell silent. Henry glanced over at the truck and noticed Ahmed was no longer standing behind the gun. The barrel smoking from its previous burst. He rushed over to the truck bed. His heart pounding. Please be reloading, he thought. Brynn provided cover fire from behind the burnt-out car, and Tremblay had moved up against the building on the left, firing down an alley. The incoming fire had almost stopped now. There were a few shots now and then. Henry peered into the truck bed and saw Ahmed slumped over the green tarp covered M-72 rockets. There was blood running down the tarp. Henry followed its path up to Ahmed. He's gone.

CRACK! A round flew past, narrowly missing Henry, slamming into the ground behind him. "SNIPER!" Brynn screamed. Henry ducked. Taking cover behind the truck. His heart pounding even faster. The smell of smokeless powder strong in the air around them. It's a smell Henry would never get sick of.

The soldiers from Heart's vehicle were scrambling for cover. CRACK! Another round. A soldier from Heart's vehicle collapses face down on the road. The machine gunner who slipped on the sharp turn. Brynn fired a short burst from her gun.

"Two hundred metres down the alley, fourth floor second window on the left!" Tremblay yelled. Brynn adjusted her LMG and fired another burst. CRACK! Another one of Heart's soldiers collapsed behind his cover. Henry moved quickly. He grabbed an M-72 from the truck and sprinted back to Brynn. She fired another burst, hitting the wall just below the sniper's window, indicating the target. Henry opened the M-72 and extended the tube. He gave it a solid tug as he always had in training. Brynn fired one more burst and then slid the LMG down to the ground and took cover. Henry stood up as fast as he ever had, raising the rocket up onto his shoulder. He aimed down the sight and pulled back on the trigger arming handle. Everything was suddenly quiet. Henry was so focused his mind had blocked all sound, even the sound of Heart's rifle firing a few covering shots. Henry pressed the trigger bar. The rocket hissed away from its tube, leaving behind a trail of smoke and heat. Henry didn't flinch at the noise of the blast. Within a second or two, the rocket reached its target, piercing the wall just below the window like knife through butter. Dust and debris flew from the window and bricks and bits of concrete fell to the ground. Henry stood standing, still aiming his now empty rocket tube at the building.

The echo of the explosion finally faded, and Henry's hearing returned. There was no more gunfire. "No more sniper," he shouted, dropping the tube on the ground. "You good?" he asked Brynn.

"Is… is Ahmed…?" she stuttered. Henry lowered his head. Brynn burst into tears and made her way to the truck. Tremblay met her there and grabbed his machine gun from her, tossing it on the front seat. Sergeant Heart made his way over to the truck, while his remaining soldiers tended to the dead and wounded.

"We're down Four Two Alpha… plus two more the sniper got," he said, lighting a cigarette. "Fucking Christ." His voice was shaky. He took a long drag from the cigarette and held it out towards Henry.

"We're down one…" Henry replied, his head down not noticing the cigarette. He motioned with his rifle to the truck.

"Could have been worse. C'mon, let's get back on the move. The troops need some rest."

STRIKE OUT

September 1st, 2020

Boston, Massachusetts

The bright floodlights of Fenway Park lit the worn-out ball field up
like day light. The subtle bump of the pitcher's mound now an entrance
into a large green tent surrounded by generators and antenna masts. Cables snaked from the tent in every direction connecting smaller tents and
old U.S. Army vehicles. Patrols of soldiers worked their ways through
the defunct ballpark in pairs, smoking and talking, their uniforms all mis-
matched. Some of the soldiers were wearing hunting camouflage, some
in American Army uniforms and others in plain dark clothing. Braden
Murphy, the commander of the New Boston Front, emerged from the
central tent and lit a cigarette. The light from the match cast shadows
across his face making his wrinkles and scars more noticeable. He
tossed the match to the ground and placed his field cap on his head as
he began to walk to the front gates of Fenway. He stopped abruptly after ten paces. He took a long drag from his cigarette and placed his right
hand on his holstered pistol. A well-used FN Five-seven with a tan body
and black slide. To his left, a pair of soldiers were sitting on a small
stack of crates that had been unloaded from a nearby truck. Braden's
hand squeezed his pistol, and then eased off. He took one more drag of

his cigarette and flicked it at the sitting soldiers with his left hand. "Get the fuck back to work!" he ordered as he stormed off towards the gate. The soldiers hopped off the crates and began carrying them into a nearby tent.

Braden arrived at the gate just as three pickup trucks pulled in. Their tires squealing to a halt. The light from the floodlights reflected off the chipped paint and bullet holes in the trucks. In faded grey paint on the doors of the trucks, the letters NBF barely visible under spattered blood. Soldiers from the front two trucks dismounted and began removing bodies from the back of the third truck. Braden's anger grew at the realization he had lost another truck as vehicles and weapons were hard to come by these days. With his two fingers on his outstretched hand, he motioned for the patrol leader to step forward. "What happened?" he grumbled. The patrol leader fumbled for words but found none. Braden looked to the soldiers unloading the bodies who had now stopped to watch what was happening. His hand slid down to his pistol holster and gripped the pistol's grip firmly. The patrol leader looked to his right making eye contact with his troops. Shocked expressions grew across their faces. THWACK! The force of the pistol smashing across his face felt like fire. The smack knocked a tooth loose and sent it flying out of his mouth, landing on the cracked pavement nearby. The patrol leader, now on the ground in pain, clutching his jaw. Braden glanced over to the others. He slowly replaced his pistol and lit another cigarette. "Find me a new vehicle!" he shouted to the group, "And you... Meet me in the HQ tent." The soldiers began scrambling to collect their things. One of them rushed over to assist the patrol leader and helped him to his feet.

"Well, what happened," Braden grumbled. His arms folded as he leaned against a table with a radio on it. The patrol leader, now with an icepack against his jaw, made his way over to a map pinned to a cork-board. He slung his AK-47 over his right shoulder and began to point to the map, his hands shaking. Braden made his way over to the table, sliding in uncomfortably close to the patrol leader.

"We turned here…" the patrol leader said, "Onto Summit Ave. in Reading." Using his index finger, he motioned the turn they had made on the map. "I believe we came under fire from a small patrol. They took out two men along with our radio," he said, clearing his throat. Braden leaned in, the smell of cigarettes bothering the patrol leader. "We…We ugh…We returned fire and searched the surrounding houses but couldn't find anyone," he said clearing his throat again. His hand a little less shaky now. He adjusted his rifle and realized that the entire tent was now listening to him speak.

"Well, go on…" Braden said, motioning to the map.

"Two days later, sir, we spotted movement here, on Joseph's Way," his hand sliding along the laminated map, bouncing over a small crease.

"We took and returned fire. O'Malley chased after the bastards into the fog. We heard some more fire and later found O'Malley's body here…" he said, pointing to a house. "We believe they took off into the woods and…" he paused, looking up to Braden. Braden's nostrils flared, but he held his composure and nodded for him to continue. "And… here is where they stole our truck…" Braden stood up and took a deep breath. As he backed up from the table, he exhaled and began to rub his chin with his left hand. The grey and red whiskers rustling under his fingers.

"Alright…" he paused still staring at the map. "Find me a new truck and get your men ready, Charlie Company is moving to Pennsylvania. It's time to pay our old friend Khalid a visit."

DEATH TAKES ITS TOLL

September 12th, 2020

Harrisburg, Pennsylvania

Two weeks had passed since Ahmed's death and it was clear that it weighed heavily on the team. Brynn and Henry had felt the loss the most, barely being able to speak to anyone let alone eat anything. Henry had spent most of the time sitting outside of the tent lines sipping on coffee and smoking the occasional cigarette. His glazed-over eyes staring straight ahead. He only ever managed a slight nod at the occasional passerby. Death had become normal and this was not the first time Henry had to deal with it, after all this was the second war he was fighting, but the hardest part about it for him was that it happened on the second patrol under his command. Colonel Howard had given One Four Delta three weeks of Rest and Relaxation after the completion of their last two operations and Henry used the time to replay the events repeatedly in his head, trying to shake the thought that it was his fault.

He thought back to the day Colonel Howard had promoted him to Captain. Henry and the rest of One Four Delta stood outside of their tent lines dressed in their usual clothing. A mix of tans and greens. Henry had managed to find a brand-new pair of tan combat boots just days prior on a patrol, and with the base laundry up and running his clothes were nice and fresh. He thought about the excitement Ahmed had for him. He was the first to congratulate him and offer to 'buy him a beer' the next time they found some. Fuck… Henry thought to himself, lowering his head.

Meanwhile inside the tent Brynn lay face down on her cot, numb to the world. She had barely moved for the past two weeks, only leaving her bed space for the washroom and the occasional bite to eat. Tremblay had tried to cheer her up a few times with his usual 'charm', but it wasn't helping, much. Her pillow stuffed inside of one of Ahmed's old t-shirts was all that was left of him now. His gear and weapon returned to the Quartermaster and his cot was empty waiting for its new occupant. Brynn sat up on her cot and looked around the tent. Tremblay sat on his cot quietly cleaning his machine gun with an old rag, a can of WD-40, a toothbrush and a dentist pick. He was whistling along to some music from his iPod. It sounded like classic rock. Brynn wiped away some tears and stood up, making her way to the door. Her MP-5, slung over her shoulder, ruffled her shirt in a way she would have used to care about correcting. Her bandaged arm was visible through her green t-shirt. She stopped for a second next to Tremblay and placed her hand on his shoulder, gave him a quick pat and headed for the door. Tremblay looked up for a second and gave her a quick nod.

William Heart made his way to the Special Operations Force Recon lines with all of his kit. His rucksack heavier than he remembered. Colonel Howard had transferred him after the way he handled the situation in Butler. As Heart passed through the concrete and HESCO walls, he walked under a plywood sign with SOFREC written in red spray paint.

He paused for a second, looking at the tent lines, taking in the view of his new home. There were four green modular tents surrounding a fifth in the centre. The command tent. He glanced quickly at the tents, looking at the signs above the doors, and began to make his way to One Four Deltas tent. As he passed the command tent, he could see Colonel Howard through the pulled-open door flap. He was pointing at a location on a map and puffing on a cigarette as he spoke to a radio operator. He made his way to his new home and saw Henry sitting out front looking down at his feet, a fresh cigarette in his hand. "Hey," he said sharply, "I thought you quit that shit."

Henry raised his head and made eye contact with Heart. He smiled slightly and nodded in reply. Heart smiled back and made his way into the tent, his rucksack snagging on the modular tent door. As he entered, Brynn was heading towards him. He smiled at her.

"Hey, I'm really sorry about…" he began.

"It's okay," she replied. "I'm sorry too." They nodded at each other and after an awkward pause; Brynn moved passed him and left the tent. Heart continued on his way to the only empty cot in the tent and dropped his rucksack on the ground. The dirt from the ground between the skid flooring puffed up in a small cloud. He laid his M4 rifle down on the cot and began removing the rest of his gear.

"Don't mind her," Tremblay said, while he continued to clean the LMG, "She just lost a boyfriend, but she'll warm up to ya. We're glad to have ya too, just like old times."

***

That night at dinner, One Four Delta sat together in the mess tent for the first time in weeks and for the first time as a new team. The tent was loud with the sounds of soldiers talking, laughing and the sizzle of burgers on the grill. It reminded Henry of his old favourite burger joint mixed with a traditional Army mess hall. Tremblay was telling an embarrassing story about their time in Afghanistan where the sound of outgoing artillery made Heart run for cover in his boxers with a pistol. Brynn burst out laughing, spitting some of her bun onto her plate. It's nice to see her smile again, thought Henry. He chuckled and took a bite of his burger.

"Fuck off it wasn't that funny!" Heart said in defense while shoving some fries in his mouth.

"Man, that… was just a couple of days before… before Max…" Henry trailed off. Tremblay lowered his burger from his mouth slowly. Heart took a sip of his drink and slowly nodded. Henry could feel the tension begin to rise at the table. He took a few fries off Heart's plate and gave him a wink. Tremblay burst out laughing with a deep belly roar. Brynn just shook her head. They grew quiet for a few more moments as they dug into their dinners. The burgers were so juicy and delicious, especially compared to the rations they had been eating for a while. They helped them escape their troubles, even if just for a few moments. Luckily for them one of the infantry battalions were able to reclaim some farming territory to the south east after a month of intense fighting with the Sabres. Now, the Federation was establishing a forward operation base in order to protect the farmers and further secure Pennsylvania. Tremblay finished his burger before the rest of the team were even close. He let out a belch and stood up with his tray. It was time for round two.

***

    Back at the SOFREC tent lines One Four Alpha was pulling in in their tan Humvee, the suspension creaking and groaning as the vehicle made its way through the potholes. It came to a stop in front of Henry and Colonel Howard. Lieutenant Frank Simmons of One Four Alpha got out of the rear passenger side, flicking a cigarette as he shut the door. He removed his helmet and nodded at Henry. Henry had met Frank back when he first transferred to SOFREC. Frank had a three-inch scar on his right cheek and when people asked how he got it, he would tell them he picked his face while high on heroine. Really, he had just fallen and cut it. After every operation, Henry and Frank would sit out front of the tent lines. They would just talk and smoke. His hair was longer than it should be now, covering his ears and flattened from his helmet. He slung his M14 battle rifle over his shoulder and made his way over to Henry. By now, Colonel Howard was on his way back to the command tent after a short conversation with Captain Fishman, the commander of One Four Alpha. The cherry red glow of Howard's cigarette visible even as he faded in the darkness. The rest of One Four Alpha dismounted the vehicle and Captain Fishman told them to get their kit to their tent and grab some food. One of them shouted that they were heading to the medic's tent, but the rest seemed to ignore him.

    Lieutenant Simmons stopped in front of Henry and lit another cigarette, the flash from the lighter lighting up his dirt-covered face. His scar under his right eye still visible through the dirt. The two talked briefly about their last operations. Colonel Howard had tasked One Four Alpha with scouting north and disrupting NBF supply movement. They were able to destroy convoy of pickup trucks carrying supplies towards Scranton. As the teams' sharpshooter, Lieutenant Simmons eliminated two high-ranking NBF officers. A small feeling of pride came over him. Henry told him what happened to Ahmed and Simmons grew quiet. Any feeling of pride he had was now gone. "Fuck... I'm sorry man," He said. Henry patted him on the shoulder and cleared his throat. Simmons pointed to the medic's tent and explained how their newest member, Corporal Martinez, had been wounded in the convoy ambush. "Martinez was struck twice by incoming rounds while laying down suppressive fire," Simmons said. "Once in the plates of his body armor and a second time in the shoulder. Fucker took it like a champ! You wouldn't even know the prick was shot." Henry laughed, and suggested Simmons get some rest, after all, they had a long couple of weeks. Simmons nodded and made his way into their tent, flicking his cigarette at Henry on his way in.

STEEL TOWN BLUES

September 21st, 2020

Pittsburgh, Pennsylvania

The sun was setting over downtown Pittsburgh and General Khalid Almasi stood in his office in the top floor of the PPG Place tower in the heart of the city. He stood close to the window, arms folded behind his back, watching the sunset. A flock of birds flew past as a convoy of Humvee's drove by on the street. His gaze stopped at the Sabre's flag flying over Fort Duquesne. A red flag with a golden sabre in the centre. A smile grew across his face for a second or so, barely seen through his thick black and grey beard. An explosion echoed out in the distance causing the birds to change course. In the room, a large oak desk sat a few feet behind him with an AK-47 resting against it, papers scattered across the desktop. The room was a large rectangle with dark wood walls, floor to ceiling windows and Sabre flags hanging on either side of the double doors. In the right corner was a private washroom. A woman with long dark hair and olive skin entered the office and made her way to the desk. Her M4 rifle slung across her back, the sling ruffling her army-green shirt barely making the name Saba visible on her chest. She stopped just short of the desk, reached into her cargo pocket of her camouflaged pants, and pulled out a folded piece of paper. "Another report sir," Saba said as she unfolded the paper. Khalid turned in place and stared at her. The setting sun silhouetting him against the backdrop of the surrounding Pittsburgh skyline. He nodded for her to continue.

"We ambushed a reconnaissance patrol in Butler and destroyed two armored fighting vehicles and we estimate about fifteen to twenty were killed," she said. Khalid smiled and unfolded his arms. He made his way over to the desk and reached for the piece of paper. "There is some bad news sir," she continued. "The platoon we sent out was almost completely eliminated… only three of them made it back." Khalid sat down in his chair, the metal springs creaking and groaning. He began stroking his beard with his other hand. He lifted another piece of paper from the desk and began reading it. The paper detailed the losses of a month-long battle to the south and a new base established by Federation forces. Khalid crumpled the report. "Sir…" Saba said. "There is also word that the NBF is making a push for Pennsylvania." Khalid's eyebrows raised as he looked up to make eye contact with Saba. "We've received some intel that they are moving a large force from Boston and are headed this way. We think they may be planning an attack on Harrisburg, but…" she paused, "I believe they plan on hitting us first." Khalid waved for Saba to leave. She nodded and turned towards the door. As she opened the door, she could hear Khalid say something under his breath, but could not quite make out what it was.

Khalid stood back up from his desk and began to pace back and forth; clenching his fists, his breathing becoming heavier and heavier. He stopped next to his desk and turned towards it. "FUCK!" he screamed as he wiped the desk clear of papers with his arms. The reports fluttered to the floor. He grabbed his AK-47 and stormed over to a chalkboard stand. It had faint markings of math problems from its former life in a nearby school. The chalkboard now listed unit counts including vehicles and soldiers on one side and supplies on the other. The unit count side listed fifty platoons of twenty to thirty soldiers each and five vehicles per platoon. Thirty-one of the platoons had large chalk white X's marked through them. Thirty-one lost platoons. Khalid picked up the piece of chalk from the tray. He forcefully slammed it against the board causing it to snap. Bits of it fell to the floor amongst a small cloud of dust. Khalid put a large X through Five Platoon. Only eighteen platoons left. Angrily, he grabbed the chalkboard and spun it to the other side. Supplies. He put an X through Seven Springs, his southeastern farm.

Khalid knew they were running out of men and food, but he could not turn back to Braden. Not after the way he betrayed him five years ago. You arrogant fool. He knew Braden was unstable. He killed a man for questioning a plan once; of course, he would kill Khalid for attempting to take over the NBF. Khalid made his way back to the window, the sun now fully set. Everything was dark except the few lights from the tents and buildings below. His breathing still heavy. His heart racing as fast as the thoughts in his head. Thoughts of how Braden took over the Republic Sabres and renamed them to the New Boston Front. Soldiers still loyal to the Republic aided Khalid in his attempt to take control. When that failed, they fortified Pittsburgh under the Republic banner. Khalid made his way back to door of his office. He opened it forcefully startling two soldiers standing guard. "Major Hadad!" he said pointing to a soldier sitting at a desk in the hall. "Get the rest of the platoons ready to deploy. We're moving out." The Major nodded and began talking away on a radio at his desk.

***

Inside a large tent at the centre of the Fort Duquesne Park, Nella Saba and the rest of Rapier Squad; a team of three men and two women, stood around a large map of Pennsylvania laid out on a table. Pointing to it, she brought her team up to speed on the location of NBF troop movement and the locations of recent battles with the Federation. The light above the map flickered. The team looked around at one another. One of the men with a bushy red beard cleared his throat. Everyone turned to look at him. He was standing with his arms folded in front of him and his RPK machine gun slung across his back. He asked what Saba was expecting them to do and why they had not received any order from General Almasi. "This OP is off the books," Saba said looking around at her team. "Khalid…" she started. "General Almasi knows we can't fight the NBF and the Federation at the same time. He's too stubborn to abandon the city and move the remaining troops to Las Vegas." Most of the team nodded. The radio on the table behind them started chattering and the team all turned their heads towards it. A Major began calling for unit leaders to meet him in an hour for orders to move. Saba looked back at the team when the Major was finished. "I'm not going to that," she said shaking her head. She pulled an elastic band out of her pocket and put her long black hair up into a ponytail. "Now…" she said hesitantly. "What I'm proposing is a Black OP to disrupt the NBF. That should allow the General time to form a real plan." The man with the beard removed his RPK from across his back and placed it on the floor.

It made a loud thud on the plywood flooring. He leaned on the table and stared at Saba. His gaze, like daggers, pierced that air between them.

"You fucking expect us to disobey him, Nells?" he asked.

"Yes Walsh. I do," Saba replied. Walsh stood back up and smiled. He waved his hand towards the map motioning for her to continue. Saba leaned in and began to detail her plan.

***

General Almasi stood in front of the remaining eighteen platoon commanders in his office. His AK-47 slung on his shoulder as a symbol that he is still a fighter. He looked around the room at his leaders. Many of them young, in their early twenties, a mix of former military, civilians and insurgents from the Middle East. The room was silent with the exception of the occasional throat clearing or cough. Saba was nowhere in sight. "Alright, listen up!" Khalid ordered. The room snapped to attention. Major Hadad was ready to take notes. "The time has come to rid this state of the Federation. We will strike hard and fast. And we will share our spoils with the NBF as a show of good will." A few of the platoon commanders looked around the room. Looks of confusion across their faces. Khalid started to move towards the window. He stared out over the Pittsburgh skyline and took a deep breath. The platoon commanders were becoming anxious. Unsure of what was going to happen. Khalid turned back to face the room. "Prepare your men," He said. "I want every soldier available ready to fight within the fortnight. A detailed plan will be disseminated to by then. DISMISSED!" The platoon commanders came to attention, driving their right feet into the floor. They all turned and headed out of the office.

"Major?" Khalid said now staring out the window. "Bring me Rapier Squad."

DECISIONS BRING CONSEQUENCES

Henry emerged from the headquarters tent after two hours of receiving orders for their next mission. He closed his notepad and tucked it into the large pocket of his brown cargo pants. He cupped his hands over his mouth and exhaled into them, the steam from his breath escaping through his fingers. The morning air was crisp as winter was drawing closer. He adjusted his scarf and made his way to his tent. As he walked, his rifle tapped subtly against his hip. He had his SCAR-L rifle ever since he met up with Tremblay at the beginning of the war. It was from Tremblay's private collection but was one of his least favourite pieces. Too flashy for his tastes, Henry thought as he pressed his hand against the body of the weapon to keep it still. Captain Fishman, the commander for One Four Alpha, pushed passed Henry and yelled for Lieutenant Simmons to come see him. Simmons burst from Alpha's tent wearing only his green cargo pants, flip-flops and a scarf. His hair messed and sticking up; a pistol in his left hand. "Pack your shit," Fishman yelled to him. "You're rolling out with Carson on Delta's next OP. They need a sniper."

Simmons smiled and pulled out a cigarette, he lit it up and nodded at Henry as he passed by. Captain Fishman disappeared into the tent grumbling about getting some sleep.

Simmons entered Delta's tent a short while later, just as Henry was getting started on their orders. He dropped his bag and body armor on the floor and sat down on it. He began playing with the bipod on his M14 as he listened to Henry. "Alright, we've received some intel that General Almasi is making a push for Harrisburg," Henry said. "It looks like they are mobilizing a force and we believe they intend to hit here." The team looked around the tent gauging each other's reactions. Tremblay managed a smirk. Henry paused and took a moment to look around the tent as well. He took note of the teams' reactions. He pointed to a section of the map north of Harrisburg with his collapsible pointer, indicating the suspected location of a new NBF base. They had all heard rumors of an NBF base near them, but this was a hard confirmation. "They appear to have a sizeable force. About a Battalion plus, moving in to our North West. We estimate they have set up camp in the locale of Penn State," Henry said.

"Let me guess, they want us to magically take them out?" Heart muttered. A hint of sarcasm lingered in the air. Tremblay laughed, welcoming the challenge. Outside the tent, a few vehicles started up and sounds of soldiers reading their weapons resonated through the tent.

"Not today Tremblay," Henry said, tapping the map with his pointer. "One Four Alpha is tasked with recon and disruption of NBF movement to the North West.". Simmons looked up to make eye contact with Henry; he was no longer playing with the rifle bipod. Alpha was supposed to be on rest. Henry explained that he had requested Simmons as an attachment for their OP before he knew Alpha was going to be heading back out. Simmons nodded in approval. Heart cleared his through as though to say to get on with the briefing. "Right," Henry continued, "Our mission is to head into Pittsburgh." Tremblay sat up straight, no longer smiling. Brynn slid off her cot onto the floor like a kid listening to a scary ghost story. "With the Sabre's making a move, we're tasked with a recon of the city and nothing more. Orders are to stay hidden and not engage."

***

Lieutenant Simmons emerged from Delta's tent just as Alpha's Humvee started to pull away. Captain Fishman gave him a nod. Simmons returned it. As the Humvee left the tent lines Martinez stood up in the turret and blew him a kiss, which Simmons caught and placed affectionately on his ass. Martinez burst into laughter and sat back down. Henry appeared next to him just as he was lighting a cigarette. His butane lighter hissed as the flame ignited the paper. "I should be going with them," he said to Henry. "How come you asked for me to be attached anyway?" he asked. Henry grabbed the chair next to him and placed it facing Simmons. He laid his rifle down on the ground and took a sip from his coffee. "I guess you didn't know Howard would send them back out," Simmons said. He took a long haul of his cigarette. He stared at the steam rising from Henry's coffee.

Henry placed the near empty coffee mug on the ground next to his rifle and took a deep breath. He exhaled slowly watching his breath dance away in the slight breeze. "I had to choose," he said. Simmons looked up at him. "I got to choose what operation we did. Originally Alpha was slated for Pittsburgh and we were going to go North." Henry stood up from his chair and grabbed his rifle, slinging it over his shoulder. "Colonel Howard left it up to me to choose which one we took. I figured North would be a good break for Alpha." Simmons asked why Henry didn't ask for another marksman after he found out that Alpha was moving out anyway. Henry moved the chair back and started head back into the tent. "Because, you're the best marksman I know. Now get your shit together, we leave at sundown." Simmons smiled and pulled out another cigarette.

***

October 2nd, 2020
F.O.B. Seven Springs, Pennsylvania

One Four Delta pulled into F.O.B. Seven Springs at two am in their black Ford truck. The engineers were working around the clock to get the walls built. Concrete highway dividers served as barricades for the main entrance. They were set up in a zig-zag pattern to stop a vehicle from building up speed and ramming the gate. A military standard. A soldier stopped them at the gate, a young private no more than twenty. He shined a flashlight into the vehicle, the light made Tremblay angry. A few feet away from the vehicle was a small make shift tower with another young soldier manning a machine gun. He was nervous and pointing the gun directly at the cab of the truck. The young private spoke into the radio briefly then moved his flashlight to the truck bed. Heart stood in the back leaning against the fifty-cal, he stared at the soldier, expressionless. Brynn was sitting down leaning against the tailgate. She smiled. The soldiers radio squawked a confirmation and he waved them into the F.O.B.

Tremblay parked the truck in front of an empty tent and said he would head to get some gas. Henry told the rest of the team to head to the kitchen tent and get some food. Colonel Howard had made sure the kitchen would be open for them when they arrived. The team each grabbed a plate of bacon and eggs and sat quietly, shoveling food into their mouths. Brynn told Tremblay to lay off the beans. He replied with a toothy bean caked grin and continued to eat. After fifteen minutes or so, the cooks began to shut the grills down and clean up, one of them grumbled about going back to bed. Henry tossed his garbage out and thanked the cooks for opening back up.

On the way back to the tent lines, Tremblay lit up a cigar he managed to buy off someone in Harrisburg. "What?" he said as the whole team looked at him. "Might be the last one for a while." Henry, Brynn and Heart made their way into the tent while Tremblay and Simmons stood outside to finish their smokes. There was some distant gunfire to the north, but the nearby generator muffled it. Once the team was set for bed, Henry unplugged the lights.

***

The pickup truck rolled quietly to a stop on the east side of Schenley Park. Tremblay tucked the keys into his pocket and headed to the truck bed where he motioned for Brynn to pass him his LMG. She passed him the gun, then grabbed her MP-5 and an M-72 rocket and hopped out of the truck, making her way into the trees nearby. Simmons removed the protective covers from the sight on his M14 and began to follow her. Heart stood standing in the bed of the truck keeping watch for any Sabres wile Henry gathered their gear. The sky was clear and the light from the moon made it easy to spot any movement coming from across the golf course in the park. Henry tapped the side of the truck and began to head towards the tree line. Heart grabbed his rifle and the last two M72 rockets from the truck and followed Henry. Once they made it to the tree line, they sat quietly for a few minutes ensuring that no one had heard them. Heart strapped one of the M72 rockets to Henry's small-pack and tapped him on the shoulder. Henry gave the signal for the team to stand up and continue. He was nervous. His hands trembled slightly. It could be from the cold. There had not been any enemy movement since they left the F.O.B. and even Tremblay seemed a little nervous. He had mentioned when they parked the truck that he was surprised they made it this far into the city unnoticed. We'll just remain vigilant, Henry thought.

As the sun began to rise, Heart quietly suggested that they look for a place to rest. Henry agreed and called the team to a halt, pulling out his map. Heart moved in next to him and suggested a subdivision across from Kennard Playground. Henry agreed again and informed the team. He folded the map up and they began to head out.

A few birds chirped in the sky as they moved through the trees. Their movement scared a small family of deer, causing the team to halt for a brief moment. For an enemy stronghold, Pittsburgh was eerily quiet. Burnt-out vehicles dotted the otherwise empty streets. After another ten minutes of slow walking, they arrived in the subdivision. This particular area had just started construction when the city was seized. Construction equipment lay strewn across dirt lawns as half-finished homes rotted and decayed. The sun was almost up so they quickly spread out and quietly checked the nearby finished townhomes. Simmons found one that overlooks the city and suggested they set up there for the day. Brynn moved up to the town home. A row of three homes facing to the west with a magnificent view of downtown Pittsburgh. The paint was faded and peeling. The majority of windows were broken or missing. Brynn, Tremblay and Heart stacked up on the slightly open door while Henry and Simmons kept watch outside. They moved in swiftly, disappearing into the home within seconds. After a minute, Brynn reappeared in the doorway and gave the thumbs up. Henry and Simmons moved in and closed the door behind them. "I'll take first watch," Simmons said heading upstairs. Tremblay was already rooting through the kitchen looking for tins of food. The home looked as if someone had just moved in. There were boxes lining the halls and furniture in odd places. Brynn sat down on the couch and a cloud of dust puffed up into the air. She tried to fight a cough. Henry moved upstairs and found Simmons sitting in a big leather chair, his M14 resting on a large desk aiming towards the city centre through a cracked window. Henry flopped down on the love seat sending a large cloud of dust into the air. "Smart," Simmons said. "Get some rest; I'll wake you when it's your watch." Henry took off his jacket and body armor and quickly fell asleep.

WAR IS HELL

October 3rd, 2020

Penn State University, Pennsylvania

A distant plume of smoke filled the air to the east. It lingered over the centre of the university as bits of rubble and fabric fall to the ground. Seconds later the sound of the explosion rattled the windows in the derelict office building that Rapier Squad was using as an observation post. Nella Saba peered through her binoculars for signs of fighting, but the crumbling buildings blocked most of the view. Distant bursts of machine guns echoed through the streets, spaced out by intermittent pops of semi-automatic rifle fire. Walsh tightened his grip on his RPK machine gun, peering through the attached flip sight for any signs of movement. "Sounds like someone is doing our job for us," he said, a smirk growing across his face. Saba smiled, glancing over at Walsh as he watched the fighting in the distance. Walsh clambered up from behind the gun and stretched. He had been laying in the prone for almost 2 hours now. Saba cringed as his back cracked. "Watch the gun for me," He said, pointing at the gun as he started to walk away. "I gotta piss."

Walsh returned a few minutes later with a meal ration in hand. Pasta sauce dripping from his beard. "Where's mine?" asked Saba. He reached into the cargo pocket of his pants and tossed a meal at her. The ration soared across the room, landing on her back and sliding to the

84

floor. She flinched. Walsh slumped down against the wall and continued to eat his meal. The sounds of his chewing echoed through the near empty room. Saba stayed in position behind the gun wincing as Walsh chomped on his food. "How can you eat that shit without complaining?" she asked. Walsh paused. He looked up from his meal and his eyes met with Saba's. He grinned a toothy grin through his beard. His teeth stained red with the red pasta sauce. "Prick," she laughed turning her head back. Walsh let out a belch that vibrated the room and tossed the now empty ration pack to the floor. He wiped his beard with his scarf as he stood up. He made his way across the room and pushed Saba out of the way, motioning for her to go eat. She slumped down where Walsh had been sitting and gagged as she opened up her meal. A cold and mushy, but congealed, blob of what was labeled as 'Cheese Tortellini'. "So… what do you think of the General?" she asked. Her pasta muffled her words.

"Huh…Almasi… The man's a fool," Walsh said matter-of-factly. Saba, taken back by his response.

"Why do you say that?" she said defensively.

"He's lost well over 100 men in the past 3 months, a major source of food and morale is low as fuck," he said.

"Yeah… well he has…" Saba started.

"And besides," he said, cutting her off. "How great can he be if his best fighters are running Ops off the books?" Saba was staring hard into her ration. Searching for a reason to disagree with Walsh. She found nothing. She mixed up her pasta and sauce slowly, sitting quietly as the tension filled the room. After a few minutes, her pasta was finished. She tossed the empty package on the floor with the other and stood up. As she made her way over to Walsh she let out a burp that made him chuckle.

"The others should be back from their recon soon," She said sitting down in her chair by the window. She picked up her binos and scanned the distance for movement.

"You know… we could just not go back," Walsh said, looking towards her. "Probably survive longer with the Federation…" he mumbled, trailing off.

***

October 4th, 2020

Penn State University, Pennsylvania

"One this is One Four Alpha… SITREP… Over," Captain Fishman whispered into the radio microphone.

"One, send," the radio operator, responded.

"One Four Alpha…" Fishman trailed off. "One Four Alpha… Enemy: unknown number of combatants at grid 5741–1878, four KIA," He paused and took a deep breath. "Friendly: At grid 5959–1769, engaged enemy, three friendly KIA and one wounded." Fishman paused again, clutching the bullet wound on his left arm. He took a deep breath and pressed the radio talk switch again. "We completed our objective but ran into an unknown enemy force on our withdrawal. Our vehicle was destroyed. Requesting immediate evac." He dropped the radio switch to his side, it hung by its cable. He dug a fresh bandage out of his vest to replace the blood soaked hastily applied one on his arm

"One, roger, wait out," the radio operator replied. Fishman took another deep breath. The short pause felt like an eternity. "One, we have an armored reconnaissance patrol about fifty klicks from your position, hold tight, out," the radio operator said firmly.

Fishman pulled the radio headset off and tossed it on the floor. He pulled a cigarette from the pocket of his tactical vest and lit it with his zippo. As he took a long haul from it, he looked around at the derelict church in which they had taken refuge. Church pews chopped up and burned for firewood in barrels scattered around the room. Books littered the floor along with garbage and clothing. The walls stained with old blood and decorated with bullet holes. Corporal Martinez pushed one of the few remaining pews up against the rear emergency exit and began leading a long wire back towards Captain Fishman. He cut the wire and handed it to Fishman. "How many claymores we got?" Fishman asked.

"Just the one. Williams had the rest..." Martinez replied. Fishman took a long drag of his cigarette and tossed it to the ground. He pulled out a clacker for the claymore from the side pouch of Martinez's tactical vest and began connecting the wires. He ordered Martinez to get some rest before relieving Jackson at the front entrance.

As Martinez slept on a pile old clothes Captain Fishman slowly walked around the church. The pain from the bullet in his arm radiated up and down his arm. It felt like a hot knife stabbing him. He checked in briefly with Private Jackson who was sitting behind a desk at the front entrance of the church. Jackson and Martinez had carried the large oak desk from the office down the hall so they would have something to sit at while keeping watch. Fishman sat down next to the young private, not more than twenty-five years old. He pulled a half-eaten chocolate bar from his vest and motioned for Jackson to take some. The private reached out with a shaky hand and grabbed the bar. He snapped off a row of three cubes and held it back out to Fishman.

"No, you keep it," Fishman said, shaking his head. He could tell Jackson was exhausted and beat down. The young private had been through hell. Three of his friends were killed hours earlier and his Captain was wounded. Now they were just sitting in a church awaiting rescue. Surrounded by god knows how many enemies. "You lads did me proud today," Fishman said attempting to reassure him. "Fuck, we must have taken out at least thirty or forty NBF troops and their vehicles."

"Think those other pricks were NBF?" Jackson asked, his eyes still scanning for movement.

"Probably… I don't think the Sabres have more than three good men left," Fishman replied with a slight chuckle. He stood up, grasping at his arm. He groaned in pain. He patted the young soldier on the back of his body armor and made his way back into the main hall.

***

Debris rained down from the ceiling as smoke escaped the building in the newly created hole in the wall. Fishman, as though everything was in slow motion, looked around the room. Martinez was shouting something to him, but he couldn't make it out. The sound of his voice muffled as though they were underwater. Even the firing of Martinez's rifle seemed quiet. As he finally rose to his feet and shook his head, he spotted Jackson. His body blown across the room from the force of the blast. Blood began pooling around him from shrapnel holes and his missing arm. A round slammed into the ground at Fishman's feet, snapping him back from his daze. He ran for cover behind a broken church pew, still struggling to make out what Martinez was shouting. The sound of incoming bullets cracked all around him. They were pinned down.

The smoke slowly cleared around the hole, blown away by the gentle breeze outside. Fishman could see a person moving towards the church. He took aim. Fired. Missed. His hands were too shaky to get a good shot. The person ducked behind an old car for cover. A muffled voice shouted from the other side of the car. More incoming fire came from the right. Martinez ducked as rounds slammed into the window frame, raining bits of the remaining glass down onto him. Fishman fired a short volley of rounds into the car to suppress his target, then he stood up to move positions. He sprinted across the room as fast as he could. Rounds continued to crack all around him. Suddenly his right leg gave out. He collapsed and slid along the floor. He managed to get into cover behind a church pew as Martinez drew the fire away. Fishman's leg burned as blood began to stain his olive-green pants from the freshly received bullet wound. Martinez continued to return fire out of the window as rounds cracked all around them. The soldier on the right moved closer, taking cover behind a parked car in the parking lot. He was a large man with a beard. The other soldier, a woman with dark messy hair, fired on Martinez's position to provide cover for her teammate.

Fishman hastily applied a bandage to his leg and attempted to stand up. The leg gave out from under him as a searing pain shot up and down the limb. He was beginning to feel dizzy from the loss of blood. "We need to fall back!" he shouted to Martinez. He tried to stand again, this time fighting through the pain, he began to move across the room.

Near the window, spent casings and empty magazines surrounded Martinez. He had managed to pull a few of Jacksons remaining magazines from his vest, but he was down to just two left. He glanced over his shoulder to Captain Fishman who was attempting to move the pew they had used to block the rear emergency door. He was struggling and loosing strength. Martinez stood up and fired a quick burst of automatic fire from his rifle. The magazine ran dry. The two soldiers outside ducked for cover behind the vehicles. Martinez turned and started to run across the room. It was silent now and the church hall was filled with the smell of smokeless powder and dust. He could hear a faint ringing in his ears from the constant firing of his rifle. He made it to the centre of the room when he heard a muffled thud and a faint vibration traveled through the floor to his foot. Corporal Martinez turned and watched as a small orb rolled towards him. An M67 fragmentation grenade. It came to a rest against a piece of wood on the floor a foot from him. "GRENADE!" he shouted. He turned and looked at Fishman. Within a second, Martinez was gone. The force of the blast knocked Fishman forward into the emergency door.

As the cloud of smoke cleared the church hall and bits of debris rained down, Captain Fishman laid motionless on the floor. He felt like he had just been kicked in the gut by a mule. His ears were ringing and both sides of his body felt like they were on fire. After a few seconds that felt like a lifetime, he coughed and began to sit up. He rested against the wall and glanced around the room. His rifle was out of reach on the floor by his feet. Martinez's torso laid face up in the middle of the room. His legs, gone. Fishman coughed again. A little blood sprayed out of his mouth. "Fuck," he said, wincing in pain. He looked over to the hole in the wall as two soldiers entered. One went right, the other, left. He began running his hands along the floor at his sides to find a weapon, a piece of wood, anything. His hands found a wire, and then something plastic. The claymore mine. One of the soldiers noticed his movements and began to move towards him. He whistled to the other soldier through his bushy red beard. The other turned. Her messy black hair fanned out behind her as she moved. As they moved towards Fishman, he pulled the plastic claymore mine onto his lap. He grabbed the clacker and held it in his hand down at his side. He toggled the safety lever off. The bearded man smiled and raised his RPK machine gun, aiming it at Fishman. "Fuck…you…" Fishman groaned. He pressed the detonator switch on the clacker. As the claymore exploded, the church filled with smoke and hundreds of steel ball bearings flew across the room.

INTO THE PITTS

Henry walked over to the couch Tremblay was sleeping on and kicked his boots, waking him up. The sun had almost set, and the team was getting ready to head into downtown Pittsburgh. Their two-day reconnaissance of the city had proven fruitful. They had watched as a large convoy of Sabre vehicles moved out of the city to the northeast. There had been very little movement within the city since. The day before, Henry and Simmons patrolled closer to the downtown core and observed a number of empty observation posts. They had scouted their best route into downtown in hopes of Colonel Howard green lighting an incursion deeper into the city. That approval came just hours before they were to return to F.O.B. Seven Springs.

Tremblay sat up on the couch and rubbed his face with both hands. The whiskers on his face crinkled and crunched as his hands ran over them. Henry walked back over with a lukewarm coffee he had heated up with a ration heater pack. A small pouch inside a plastic bag that creates a chemical exothermic reaction when water is added to it. Tremblay inhaled the aroma of the instant coffee. He took a sip and sighed a sigh of enjoyment. "We rolling out soon?" Tremblay asked. Henry nodded yes through a yawn. "Good," Tremblay replied. "I'll help Heart with the flares when I'm done this drinking this shit."

Henry grabbed two more lukewarm coffees and made his way upstairs. Brynn was sitting in the large leather office chair while Simmons was showing her how to adjust the sights on his M14. The battle rifle had been Frank Simmons best friend since he transferred to SOFREC. It was a heavy beast, close to fifteen pounds, but he loved it. He would constantly turn down other options over the versatility he claimed his M14 had. Henry walked over slowly and placed the coffees on the desk. It's nice to see Brynn smiling again, Henry thought to himself. Simmons thanked him for the coffee, but said he never touches the stuff. Henry took the cup back. Thank god, it was the last coffee. Brynn and Simmons switched places, so she could drink her coffee. She asked Henry what the plan was. He paused, then took a long sip of his coffee. "Well, we're a go for heading into town," he said before taking another sip. "Once Heart has finished disabling the trip flares and we've got our shit together we'll move out." Brynn looked over at Simmons who was scanning the distance through the sight on his rifle. She asked if the plan was just to recon the area for an assault on the city. "To start," He replied. "We've also been tasked with observation of troop movements and locating high value targets. But…" he paused, sipping his coffee again. "But we'll need to play it by ear. There are a ton of unmanned OP's out there, so we'll need to keep an eye out for booby traps and roving patrols." Henry finished the last of his coffee. The bitter taste of the black instant military ration coffee lingered in his mouth. He stood up and placed his empty cup on the desk. He slapped Simmons on the back and headed back downstairs.

***

Cricket chirps echoed off the buildings surrounding Penn Avenue. They stopped as the team grew close and started up again once they had passed. Henry looked around at the garbage that littered the streets. "Keep your eyes peeled for IED's," he whispered to Tremblay who was a few feet in front of him. Tremblay gave a quick thumbs up over his shoulder as he slowed his pace a little. They had not seen another living soul since they made their way into downtown Pittsburgh. Strange for a fortified enemy base. Along the sidewalks, bodies had been stacked like sandbags. Most of them decayed, but a few were more recently deceased. Most likely executed soldiers or civilians who refused to help the Sabres. Henry gagged as he glanced at a crow picking at one of the more recently deceased bodies. Watching through his night vision goggles added a layer of unease to the scene. The world lit up in an eerie green glow. A brief gust of wind blew down the street towards them picking up dust and light trash from the road. The stench of the bodies penetrated their nostrils as some trash swirled around their feet. Henry pulled his scarf up over his mouth and nose. It didn't help much. The moonlight bounced off the few remaining windows in the build-ings as the shadows danced around it. Tremblay veered the team to the right as they came across a perfectly good Humvee in the centre of the intersection ahead. They moved in an old convenience store near the intersection and set up an all-around-defense, watching for movement. After a few minutes, Henry opened his bag and grabbed his map, a red flashlight and his ranger blanket to hide the light. He tapped Simmons on the shoulder and motioned for him to come look at the map under the blanket. "I think we should head out back and skirt around the city, along Fort Duquesne Boulevard as planned." He said to Simmons, who nodded in agreement.

"I think we should establish an observation post in the old Wyndham hotel…here," Simmons pointed to the hotel on the map. "That'll give us good line of sight to the tower and surrounding areas, and possible exfil routes here and here."

Henry agreed and turned the light off and pulled the blanket off them. After he packed everything away, he quietly briefed the team. "Alright, here's the plan," He whispered. "We'll head out back to the ally and move down 6th to Fort Duquesne Boulevard. Once we hit One Gateway Centre, we'll move through the courtyards to the old Wyndham hotel where we'll set up shop." The team, all maintaining watch, nodded in unison. Henry tapped Tremblay twice on the boot to signal they were ready to move. Tremblay quietly stood up and moved to the rear door. The rest of the team followed.

As they made their way down Fort Duquesne Boulevard the faint rumble of generators bounced off the buildings. The sound growing steadily louder as they moved forward. Henry slowly turned to look behind him. Brynn was scanning the upper levels of the buildings on her left. Behind her was Simmons followed by Heart who would occasionally turn around and scan the rear. They came to a halt when they reached Stanwix Street. Tremblay crouched at the corner of the building. Henry moved up close behind him and they peered around the corner at the same time. Three hundred metres down Stanwix, there was a checkpoint with two guards smoking under a pale light. The sandbag walls were about chest high with a small plywood hut on one side.

Just beyond that, the PPG Place tower stood out like a lighthouse. The top ten floors were lit up like it was business as usual with random lights on the lower floors. Henry scurried across the street and posted up next to the other corner. He aimed his rifle down the road. The crosshairs of his ACOG sight painted directly on the side of the head of one of the guards. Brynn moved in behind Tremblay and kicked his boot. He stood up and shuffled quickly across the road. One by one, they crossed the intersection. Once the whole team crossed, they took a quick listening pause. Lieutenant Simmons aiming his rifle down the road towards the guards. All right... we're good to go, Henry thought. He signaled to stand up and move on. They continued quietly as the hum of generators grew louder.

***

The inside of the Wyndham Hotel was eerie and dark. The floors littered with luggage, garbage, spent casings and bodies. The stench was foul. As the wind blew through the broken and missing windows, it would cause doors to creak. Henry's heart was pounding so bad he thought the whole team could hear it. He glanced behind him and could tell everyone was on edge. They were officially in the heart of enemy territory. At any moment, they could run into a Sabre patrol. We'd be fucked, Henry thought. His heart now in his throat. Suddenly a loud clinking noise rang out behind them. They all swiveled in place. Heart, Simmons and Brynn took a knee. No movement. They scanned the hotel lobby they had just passed through. Another clink! They all swiveled in place, aiming their weapons towards the front desk. Heart stood up and took a few steps forward. He lowered his rifle.

"The wind blew some casings off the desk," he whispered.

Henry relaxed his aim and breathed a sigh of relief. As he turned around, he noticed Tremblay was grinning.

"You're a bitch," Tremblay chuckled.

"Fuck off. It got you too. Now get the fuck upstairs," Henry retorted, quietly but firmly.

They reached the twentieth floor of the hotel after a grueling climb up the stairs. The entire team was struggling to catch their breath. Henry motioned for Brynn, Heart and Tremblay to start clearing rooms to the west while he and Simmons cleared to the east. One by one, they cleared the rooms, and every room was the same, empty. They all met back at the centre stair well. "What do we got?" Henry asked.

"All clear up here," Heart replied.

"We've got some tent lines down in the fort with a couple lights on. No movement," Brynn said.

"Good. Simmons and I will set up our post in the South-East corner room watching the tower. Heart take Brynn and set the trip flares up at the southern and centre stairwells. Trembles, barricade the northern stairwell," Henry ordered. They all took off to their respective tasks.

***

A couple hours had passed now, and Henry began to check on everyone. They only had enough food and water for another day or so and even though the patrol had been otherwise uneventful, the mess of downtown Pittsburgh was enough to give even the most hardened soldiers a nightmare or two. Henry wandered down the main hall where

Tremblay had created a fire position for his machine gun to cover the stair wells at the opposite end of the building. Henry tapped him on the shoulder and asked if he needed relief. Tremblay held up an old Gatorade bottle he found on the floor that he since filled with urine. He smirked at Henry. As he made his way back down the hall, Henry chuckled. He moved into the South-Western room where Brynn and Heart were watching the tent lines in the fort. "Any movement?" he asked. Heart shook his head no, as he lowered his night vision googles. He pointed down to the centre of the old fort and told Henry that a Humvee pulled up about an hour ago, but it had parked behind a tent and they couldn't see how many soldiers got out. Henry glanced around the room for Brynn. She was asleep on the bed in the corner, her ranger blanked laid out on top to keep her away from the dust. He was about to take over for Heart when Simmons called to him over their personal radios.

Henry made his way back to the South-Eastern room at a quick pace. He pulled an office chair next to Simmons who was peering through the sight on his rifle. "What do we got, Frank?" Henry asked. The lights had turned on in the large office in the top floor of the building. Frank Simmons was scanning the floor through the sight on his rifle. Henry grabbed the set of binoculars off the desk and raised them to his eyes. Through the binoculars, Henry scanned for movement. Another light flicked on in the top floor and caught his attention. He adjusted his grip on the binos and scanned the newly lit room. It appeared to be a standard office, nothing fancy. Grey walls surrounded grey and white desks. Instead of the usual hotel style art and pictures of people's families, the walls were dressed in Sabres flags.

"I've got movement in the main office," Simmons whispered. Henry darted his gaze back to the main office, a large rectangular shape room with dark wood walls. Large Sabre banners hung from floor to ceiling. There was a man standing with his back to the window, arms folded behind him. Simmons tightened his grip on his rifle. The reticle hovering over the man's back. His head turned slightly and exposed a thick black beard that ended at his neckline.

Henry took a deep breath. We've got to make sure it's him. We can end this. The man stepped forward to the desk and unfolded his arms. He pulled out the large black chair and sat down. Simmons flipped his weapon from safe to fire. He took a deep breath. The man in the office picked up a stack of paper and began reading. He started to comb his left hand through his beard. "Take the shot," Henry ordered. He knew they shouldn't. Orders were to stay quiet and observe. But Henry had a chance, a real chance to end the Sabres. TAK! The sound of Simmons suppressed M14 firing echoed in the room. The 7.62 millimetre round flew across the sky. Within seconds, the round pierced the glass of the office window and found its home in the back of the man's skull. A quick puff of pink mist sprayed the air just above his head before the man slumped on to the desk. Simmons exhaled. He flipped his rifle back to safe. We need to move now! Henry thought. He packed the binoculars into his bag and grabbed his rifle. He began to imagine the flak he would take for this. Howard was a good man who trusted Henry to not stray from his mission. There would be charges in his future for sure. He radioed for Heart to pack up the trip flares and get ready to move. He made his way to Tremblay to help remove a door barricade, so they could leave through the northern exit.

Henry's personal radio earpiece sprang to life with static. He started to head back to the sniping position when Brynn rounded the corner. "We've got some movement down in the tent lines," she said. Henry changed direction and began to follow her to her over watch position. "It started just a few seconds ago. I'm not sure if they heard the shot, or were told, but we need to go," she said with a slight panic to her voice. She handed Henry the binoculars. Down in the centre of the tent lines, Henry observed people beginning to scramble. A group of three soldiers hopped into a Humvee and took off towards PPG Place Tower. He passed the binos back to Brynn as Simmons burst into the room. He informed Henry and Brynn that some soldiers just discovered the body. "I'll tell Heart to leave the flares," said Brynn. The sun was beginning to rise now, and their night vision goggles would make it hard to see. Henry helped them quickly pack them away.

The four of them made their way to Tremblay who had cleared the debris from a stairwell at the north end. "Alright…" Henry said. "The plan is to book it across Fort Duquesne Bridge and make our way North-East. After a couple klicks we'll cross the river again and head back to the truck," he said, looking around at the team. They were all listening intently. "If…" he started. "If we get separated, make your way back to the truck as best you can." They all nodded. Heart helped Tremblay put on his small pack and they all headed down the stairs.

Brynn exited the door to the lobby level first. She aimed down the hallway to the South, scanning for movement with her MP-5. As the rest of the team entered the lobby area, they could begin to hear muffled shouting and footsteps to the South. Brynn tightened her grip. Tremblay set up his LMG on an overturned table next to her. Simmons and

Heart made their way to the exit and scanned for movement outside. They signaled a thumbs up to Henry. "Let's go!" Henry whispered to Brynn and Tremblay.

Heart and Brynn rushed out into the street. They took cover behind an old car and scanned for movement at the fort. Simmons, Tremblay and Henry sprinted out from the building and headed towards the bridge. After fifty metres, they stopped to provide cover for Brynn and Heart. As Brynn began to move, a bright flash emanated from a window in the top floor of the hotel. Fuck. They found our position, Henry thought. Brynn stopped and turned to look just as a Humvee with a fifty-caliber mounted machine gun rounded the corner. She froze. Fire spewed from the barrel of the gun as the gunner let loose a burst. The cracking and zipping of the rounds from the machine gun snapped her from her daze. She fired a quick returned burst from her MP-5 and sprinted for cover. Tremblay, Simmons and Henry provided suppressing fire to cover their withdrawal. Simmons lined up a shot. BLAM! The gunner on the fifty-cal collapsed into the vehicle. The Humvee skidded to a stop and the doors flew open as the soldiers began to dismount. They fanned out and took cover behind derelict cars. One of them ran behind the Humvee. Tremblay fired a long burst from his LMG. Another Sabre soldier dropped. Wounded, he squirmed to take cover, his screams could be heard slightly over the gunfire. Brynn passed Henry and took cover behind an overturned delivery truck. Henry continued to suppress the soldiers. One soldier emerged from behind the Humvee holding something on his shoulder. A long black and brown tube with an olive-green rocket on the end.

"RPG!" Simmons screamed.

The rocket shot out of the launcher and screamed down the street, kicking up dust and garbage as it went. Heart was running as fast as he could to get to cover, his blood pumping so hard he could feel it in his ears. The rocket landed in the centre of the road and its explosion sent debris into the air. As the debris rained down on him, Henry scanned the dust. Where's William? He thought. Where the fuck is William! Heart burst through the smoke and dust and sprinted by Henry. Thank fuck. Brynn was now firing her MP-5 through the clearing smoke to provide covering fire. Simmons moved back to her position and was quickly checking over Heart for wounds.

Henry and Tremblay sprinted towards the bridge. They needed to get across as fast as they could. Henry boosted Tremblay over the shoulder high concrete guardrail to bridges on ramp. Rounds continued to crack all around them. Tremblay reached down and pulled Henry up. A bullet slammed into Tremblay's shoulder, knocking him to the ground. "FUCK!" yelled Tremblay. He grabbed his left shoulder as he sat up. "You fucks!" Henry fired a few rounds in return. His magazine now empty. As he reloaded, he could hear the fifty-caliber machine gun spring back to life. Another Humvee had moved up on the right and had pinned down the others. "Let's deal with these fucks and go home," Tremblay grumbled standing himself back up. He placed his LMG on the guardrail and peppered the second Humvee with automatic fire. Henry joined in with rapid semi-automatic fire. With the second gun suppressed, Simmons, Heart and Brynn made their move to the bridge. Henry reloaded. The firing from the LMG echoed off the surrounding concrete structures. "Reloading!" Tremblay shouted as the LMG ran dry. Henry continued to lay down suppressing fire and watched as the others made their way towards his position.

A group of soldiers emerged from the hotel and fired a volley at them. The rounds whizzing and zipping by as they ricocheted off the ground by Brynn's feet. Her heart was pounding as she ran as fast as she could. Simmons grabbed Brynn by the shoulder and pulled her to the right. The second Humvee was moving into position to cut off their escape. "We won't make it to the bridge!" Simmons shouted into his radio. They took cover behind the trailer of a transport truck and motioned to Henry that they would head the other way. Tremblay fired a burst at the Humvee, killing the gunner as the vehicle drove across the grass of the park. The group of soldiers from the hotel continued to fire on Henry and Tremblay as the others withdrew. Tremblay fell back to the lower level of the bridge to cover Henry. Henry stayed in place. Chips of concrete tore off the guardrail and danced through the air as incoming rounds continued to slam into it. The soldiers were advancing faster now. No one was suppressing them.

Once Henry lost sight of the others down an alleyway, he turned and ran toward Tremblay. His heart was pounding as he ran at full sprint. He jumped and slid over the hood of a car, losing his footing on the other side. He tumbled to the ground. As he moved to stand up, a burst of machine gun fire flew by him. Tremblay cheered as he dropped a soldier that was climbing over the guardrail. Henry took a deep breath and stood back up. He made his way to Tremblay and took up a firing position next to him. He propped his rifle on the trunk of the car. His breathing was heavy. "Keep going!" Tremblay yelled. "I'll keepum suppressed!" Henry turned and continued down the bridge. He had made it halfway down when the LMG stopped firing. His heart began to sink.

He slowed his pace and turned around. Tremblay was running towards him at full tilt. His LMG pointing directly up in his right hand as he ran. Henry smiled and turned to continue across the bridge. CRACK! Henry flinched as a round soared over his head. ZIP! Another round skipped off the ground next to his feet. He turned to return fire just as a round slammed into Tremblay's back. A puff of dust created a small cloud behind him as he fell to the ground. The LMG tumbled and came to a stop a few feet from Tremblay's outstretched hand. Henry froze. His heart pounding. His ears ringing. He tried to shout to Tremblay, but his mouth wouldn't form the words. He looked back where they came from as four soldiers were taking up firing positions at the entrance to the bridge. He lined up his sight on an advancing soldier. He squeezed the trigger. The rifle kicked back, but Henry barely noticed. The soldier dropped. Another one grabbed the downed soldier and dragged him to cover behind a dusty red sedan. By now, Tremblay was standing up, staggering to make it to his machine gun. THWACK! A shot to the back of his right leg. Tremblay dropped to his knees. SMACK! A final round passed through the back of his head creating a brief puff of pink. His body sank to the ground as blood seeped from his wounds and began to pool around him.

"Jo...Jo... JONATHAN!" Henry screamed. Henry flipped his rifle to fully automatic and held the trigger. The soldiers dove for cover. Within a couple of seconds, his magazine was empty. He pressed the mag release switch and dropped it on the ground. Before it even hit the ground, he was loading another one. As he aimed at the soldier's positions, he saw another soldier appear from behind a pickup truck on the left with an RPG. Fuck! Henry turned. The rocket screamed away from its launcher and slammed into the ground next to Henry's cover seconds later. The force of the blast knocked Henry off the bridge into the river.

***

Henry coughed as he regained consciousness. Everything was dark. The faint hum of a nearby generator was the only sound Henry could hear besides his own heartbeat. He attempted to move, but his entire body ached. He groaned in pain. He tried to move his hands, but they were bound together by plastic flexi cuffs behind his back. He slid his bare right foot back and it pressed against the foot of a wooden chair. Behind him, the sound of a large zipper briefly drowned out the humming generator. Footsteps moved across the temporary plywood flooring and grew louder as they approached. The flooring bowed as the footsteps moved passed him. They came to rest right in front. He looked up, but everything was still dark. Someone removed the blindfold from his face allowing the light to blind him for a couple of seconds. He blinked rapidly. His eyes trying to adjust to the not so well-lit tent. In front of him, an older man with a thick grey and black beard sat on the edge of a large map table. His forest pattern camouflage clothes in pristine condition. On each shoulder was the Sabre's flag. He lit a cigar and took a long puff of it. He held it out in front of him and watched the smoke float away. "Your friend had exquisite taste," the man said. "It's a shame the other ones were soaked in blood." The man stood up slowly and turned to his right placing the cigar on an ashtray on the map table.

He quickly turned back to the left with a cocked fist and drove it into Henry's jaw. The man screamed, "Where's Nella Saba!" Spit flew from his mouth and found a home in his beard. Henry's vision blurred from the hit. The room spun. He spit some blood out onto his lap. He stared at the bearded man as his vision returned to normal.

The tent flap behind Henry flew open shining the bright sunlight into the tent. For a moment, Henry was able to get a better view of the tent. There was a row of cots on each side, four that he could see. He assumed there were more behind him. He was able make out the names on the barracks boxes at the foot of the cots. Two in particular, Saba and Walsh. "General Almasi…" a soldier said as he walked passed Henry, clutching a piece of paper. He passed it to the bearded man. The man stood up and grabbed the cigar from the table. He took a long puff. He held it out with his left hand this time and stared at Henry. His gaze was piercing. He stepped forward and drove his fist into Henry's jaw for a second time. Henry and the chair tipped to the right, landing hard on the makeshift flooring. As Henry drifted in and out of consciousness, he could hear General Almasi order his men to mount up and head to Penn State. Then, everything went black.

WHEN IN THE DARK, FOLLOW THE LIGHT

Date, Unknown

Location, Unknown

A voice called out to Henry. It trembled in fear as it called his name. Henry turned around in a circle. He couldn't pin point the direction of the voice. Everything was black. The voice called again, this time from behind him. Henry turned to see a green tent flap surrounded in a smoky haze. As he moved towards it, an explosion went off perforating the tent with shrapnel holes. Henry shut his eyes. His ears, ringing. As he began to slowly open his eyes, he was temporarily blinded by the bright light of the desert sun. The desert heat felt warm on his ice-cold face. Doc Taylor ran past him in a hurry. Henry turned. Confused, he followed the medic. "Doc?" he asked. Taylor ignored him as he crouched down over a wounded soldier who was screaming in pain. "Fields?" Henry paused. "What the fuck?" He spun in place to find himself standing in the centre of Outpost Nal in Afghanistan. He walked towards the tower he was positioned in when they came under fire in 2008. The gunfire was intense. As he walked up the steps, an echoed voice called out to him from inside of the tower. "You fucking killed me!" He stopped at the top step and stared at Joshua Maxell, who was laying on the floor, blood pulsing from the gaping hole in the back of his head. He could see himself, gathering ammo for the machine gun. "You killed me. Like you killed Ahmed and Tremblay," the voice said again. Suddenly, Maxwell's head turned and stared right at Henry with glaring white eyes. His heart felt like it had stopped as a pain pierced his chest. He dropped to his knees, clutching his chest as the pain radiated through his upper body. As he looked up, time slowed down. He could see himself standing behind the machine gun. He looked out to the fields. He could see a bullet flying towards the other version of himself. The air warping behind it like something from a video game. He choked back a large wad of spit as he watched the bullet slammed into the chest of his other self.

Henry shot up, awake. His heart pounding so hard it nearly leapt from his chest. He was drenched in sweat to the point he looked as if he had just climbed out of a pool. Turning to sit on the edge of his cot, Henry placed his bare feet on the cold cement floor of his cell. They made a light slapping sound as they splashed a puddle that had formed on the floor. He placed his head in his hands and wiped the cold beads of sweat from his forehead. He let out a scream as he broke into tears.

The cell was dark and cold with a dampness to it that pierced to the bone. A small dimly lit room of maybe six feet by six feet, at least by his barefooted pace. It was furnished only with a cot, a toilet and a single light caged to the ceiling. It had been Henry's home for longer than he can remember now. He kept count of the days at first, by scratching at the wall with a fingernail but, the days managed to blend together now, and his fingers were raw and bloody. He blamed it on the lack of natural light and the fact that the incandescent light bulb in the ceiling never shut off, but deep down, he knew it was because he was giving up. The sinking feeling in his gut had become constant. It was an awkward mix of hunger and hopelessness that ate away at him a little piece at a time.

Henry glared at the light in the ceiling, it was maybe a forty-watt bulb, that was wrapped in a grey metal cage of four little bars that met in the middle and crowned with a poorly placed weld in the centre. Sometimes he stared until his eyes would burn with pain. Other times, just long enough to count the bars, again. He could tell you which bar was longer than the others, but he still had no idea how long he had been in this room. Occasionally he would hear footsteps, or the odd spoken word outside the door to his cell. A solid heavy metal door with no window or bars. Even less occasionally, the door would open and a balaclava clad soldier with an AK-47 slung over his shoulder would drop a tray of some grey goopy porridge on the floor. Henry would stare at it until the soldier left, and then, eat the floor-porridge faster than he's eaten anything before.

***

January 7th, 2021
Pittsburgh, Pennsylvania

A guard shoved Henry with the butt of his gun, forcing him down the long dark hallway. A large man, the same height as Henry, but more muscular. His face covered in a bushy beard. He had a large scar across the right side of his face and he was missing the top of his right ear. An MMA fighter perhaps? Maybe in another life. Another guard walked in front of Henry. A female, with her black hair tied back in a bun. Henry couldn't see her face, but he knew she had to be beautiful. They marched down a series of what seemed like an unending maze of damp hallways. They passed two guards who nodded at the female soldier. As they passed by, one guard pretended to punch Henry in the stomach. They laughed as he flinched. The female guard in front of Henry stopped and pulled open a door to a washroom and motioned for him to go in. Henry stared at her as he walked passed. He wondered why she had her face covered with a bandana, but quickly shifted his thoughts to the washroom. Jesus did he ever need a shower. The two guards followed him into the room, shutting the door behind them. As he stopped in the centre of the room, he stared at his reflection in the dirty mirror on the wall. His blood shot eyes stared back at him, examining his black and grey unkempt beard. The room had an awful smell that had a way of embedding itself in your nostrils. It was a mix of urine and rotting rat carcasses.

Henry turned around. His hands bound in flex cuffs that were too tight on his wrists. The female guard stepped forward and pulled a knife from the front of her vest with her left hand. She had her M4 rifle slung behind her back. "Where the fuck am I?" Henry grumbled. The woman looked Henry deep in the eyes. She raised her right hand and placed her index finger over her bandana-covered lips. The woman's shush was quiet and faint. Henry gulped.

The woman reached down with her knife and cut the flex cuffs off Henry's wrists. He noticed she was missing her ring finger on her left hand but didn't pay too much attention to it. The cuffs fell to the floor with a quiet slap that echoed through the tiled washroom. As Henry rubbed his bruised wrists, he stared at his dirty hands. They trembled from his lack of strength. It had been months since he had a proper meal, so he was weaker than normal. He could feel it throughout his entire body. Henry turned around and began to wash his face in the sink. The warm water trickled through his beard. He ran the water over his hands and attempted to remove the dirt that had built up over who knows how long. He looked around for some soap, but there was none. He cleared his throat. His voice, raspy. Henry turned back around to ask for soap and saw the female guard had pulled her bandana down exposing her face. She had a scar on her left cheek that extended past her ear. She was a beautiful as he had imagined. Her olive skin was flawless despite the scar, and her green eyes gleamed, even in the poor light of the washroom. He glanced over her shoulder to the guard at the door who was peering through the slightly open door down the hallway. He told the woman to hurry up through clenched teeth behind his bushy beard. "Working on it," she replied. The woman unslung her M4 from her shoulder and turned to the door. Henry confusedly asked who they were. "I'm Saba, this is Walsh. Now let's go," the woman said. Saba? How do I know that name? Henry thought. He shook his head, flicking beads of water about the room. He dried his hands on his dirty ragged shirt as he moved back towards the door.

Walsh aimed a suppressed MP-5 down the hallway while Saba exited the room followed closely by Henry. After a few seconds Walsh fell in behind them, his boots splashed a puddle from a leaky pipe overhead. Who are these people? Henry thought as he tailed Saba. He posted up behind her as she crouched at a corner. His knees creaked as he squatted down. They always had been a little worse for wear, but in his current state, he was dreading standing back up. The hallway lights flick-ered. The hum of the lights bounced off the walls. Saba motioned back to Walsh that there were two soldiers at the end of the hallway. Their voices bounced off the walls. They were talking about something they found funny, but Henry couldn't make out what. Walsh stepped forward and leaned over Saba's shoulder. They both took a deep breath. TAK! TAK! Two rounds flew down the hallway from their suppressed guns, coming to a rest in the soldiers. They collapsed onto the floor.

The three of them quickly moved down the hallway, reaching the dead guards within seconds. Henry knelt down to grab the guard's weapon. An AK-47 slung across his chest. He rolled the guard over. It was Joshua Maxwell. Fucking Christ! Henry fell backwards, slipping in a pool of blood. Saba whispered for him to 'hurry the fuck up'. He shook his head and reached for the AK-47. His hand trembled as he unbuckled the sling. As he pulled some magazines from the guards' vest and slid them into his pockets, he stared at the man's face. He was a young soldier with a similar to build to Henry's old friend Maxwell. However, this wasn't Maxwell. Henry rose to his feet and fell in behind Saba. He struggled at first to raise the rifle, his arms were weak. His stomach rumbled with hunger pangs that felt like a knife sliding into his gut.

They continued down the hallway until they reached a grey metal door. Like the door to his cell, but this door housed a small rectangular window illuminated with the bright light from outside. The light bounced back and forth as a shadowy figure moved on the other side of the door. The air grew colder as they got closer. Walsh pushed past Henry as Saba pulled her bandana back up over face. They opened the door quickly, surprising the guard standing there. Walsh landed a punch to the guards' face with his gloved fist, followed up by another fist to the gut. The guard dropped as Walsh unsheathed his knife and drove it into the guard's throat. He dragged the body back inside and pulled his boots off. He tossed them to Henry and told him to hurry up. Henry hadn't even realized he was bare foot until now. He knelt down and slipped the boots on. They were still warm. A thought that instantly made Henry feel uneasy. Once he had the boots on Saba helped him with the dead guards' coat.

Outside of the building, the wind howled. Blowing snow across the near empty parking lot. The cold wind pierced the skin on Henry's face like tiny shards of glass. He covered his face with the neck of the coat, it helped, a little. They moved across the snow-covered lot into the street. There had not been a vehicle by in a while and Henry struggled to move through the fresh snow. He wished he had taken the guards' socks too. The cold chilled him to his core. The three moved towards the bridge leading to Fort Pitt Tunnel. The crunching snow under his feet kept him on edge. He hoped the wind was loud enough to cover the sound. The snow swirled around making it hard to see as the flakes twirled about the air in front of Henry's face. As they made their way across the bridge a truck slowly emerged from the tunnel. Henry quickly took cover behind a concrete highway divider. He watched as Saba and Walsh kept moving towards the vehicle. He slowly stood up and began to move towards the approaching truck. Walsh motioned for him to hurry up. As he approached the front of the black Ford pickup truck, the driver waved. Heart? Henry stared through the icy glass of the windshield trying to gather his thoughts.

"How'd the MP-5 work out for ya?" Brynn said from the back of the truck. She was bundled up in a white parka and goggles. Henry stared up at Brynn, he could still make out her smile, even through her winter layers. Still, he was confused. He couldn't figure out what was happening. How did they find me?

"Like a dream," Walsh said, answering Brynn. He tossed the subma-chine-gun up to her before he climbed into the truck bed. Brynn caught the gun and laid it down in the truck bed. She smiled at Henry.

"I'll explain later," Saba said, holding the rear door of the truck open. She motioned to Henry to get in. Henry climbed into the warm cab of the truck and patted Heart on the shoulder.

"Hey lover," Heart said.

"Fuck it's good to see you."

He breathed a deep sigh of relief as Saba climbed into the front seat.

"Where's Frank?" Henry asked. Heart cleared his throat as he tight-ened his grip on the steering wheel and shifted the truck into reverse. An awkward tension filled the cab. The off-road tires slipped in the deep snow, but eventually found their footing. Heart maneuvered around a snow-covered car and headed back into the tunnel.

"Get some rest," Saba said, "I'll explain everything later."

TRUST GAINED

January 17th, 2021

Harrisburg, Pennsylvania

Henry emerged from the medic's tent and zipped up his coat. The
cold January air stung as it made its way to his lungs. He had spent nearly ten days under medical supervision and the medical officer finally gave
him the all clear to head back to his tent lines, but his first stop would
be the mess tent. Must drink coffee, he thought. His winter boots that
Brynn brought him kicked the fresh powdered snow up like dust. It
reminded him of the fine baby powder like dust in Afghanistan. As he
walked down the roadway, a convoy of Humvees and Military trucks
drove passed him, forcing him into the snowbank. He examined each
vehicle as they drove by. He wondered why they were so many of them.
He counted nearly forty vehicles in total. As he was staring, he caught a
glimpse of a soldier standing behind a fifty-caliber machine gun in one
of the Humvees. His heart skipped a beat as the soldier waved to him.
It's Ahmed! Henry's hands began to shake. He stood frozen in place.
The soldier turned back to face the front of the vehicle column as he
pulled his scarf up over his light brown face. Henry took a deep breath
in. And out. In. And out. His heart rate started to return to normal

as he realized that it wasn't actually Ahmed and his brain had just been playing a nasty trick on him, again. He rubbed his cold shaky hands together as he moved back onto the road. Time for that fucking coffee.

***

Laughter emanated from the One Four Delta tent as Henry walked up to the entrance. The familiar green tent under the SOFREC sign always made him feel safe. He tucked the chocolate chip muffin he snagged from the mess tent into his coat pocket and took a sip of his coffee. As he looked over at the One Four Alpha tent, something seemed off. The door flap was unzipped and fluttering back and forth in the wind and the snow had not been cleared from the entrance in a while. They're probably out on an operation, he thought. Henry reached down and unzipped the door flap to his tent. The heat poured out, blasting him in the face. The laughter stopped as he stepped into the tent. He stood up straight and saw everyone was staring at him. After a long pause that felt like an eternity, they cheered and began to clap. Brynn walked over and gave Henry a hug. Smiling, she made her way back to her cot. Heart and Simmons smiled as they got up to shake his hand. Henry looked over towards Ahmed and Tremblay's cots. A larger man and a woman now occupied them. "Thank you," he said to them. They both nodded a slight nod back. Henry took off his jacket and sipped on his coffee as he walked over to his cot. As he sat, he let out a relaxed sigh. Home.

The two new soldiers walked over to Henry and stood at the foot of his cot. "I'm Nella Saba," the female soldier said. "And this is Aaron Walsh." Henry stared at the missing piece of Walsh's ear as he stood there. Henry kicked off his boots and asked them why he had not seen them before. He did his best to keep eye contact with them, but his gaze kept finding its way to their scars. After all, they still looked fairly new and Henry knew they had them before they rescued him. "Well…" Saba started. She paused and cleared her throat. "That's because we used to be Sabres." Henry's right hand began to shake. His coffee sloshed back and forth in the cup. Saba motioned to the end of the cot for permission to sit. Henry didn't answer. He was still trying to process what she had just said to him. She slowly sat anyway, moving his jacket over. "We were part of Spec-Ops team called Rapier Squad tasked with almost the same thing you do here," she said. Simmons muttered something under his breath and quickly left the tent. Henry watched as he fumbled with the tent door zipper. Saba continued, "When we realized the General Almasi was starting to lose it, we decided to attempt an off the books OP." Henry looked over at Walsh who was standing at the foot of his cot, arms folded across his chest. "We thought the NBF might make a play for Pittsburgh and the General thought otherwise," she said. Henry asked them what happened on that operation. Saba paused again as she searched for the words. "We were going to sabotage NBF troop movements in Penn State when we came under fire from a group of soldiers. They killed four of my team," she said.

Walsh cleared his throat. "We uh… we took them out," he said quietly. Henry noticed that Brynn and Heart were cleaning their weapons, trying not to pay attention to the story. "It turns out they were Federation guys. A small team," Walsh said. A puzzled look decorated Henry's face as he tried to figure it out. No, Not Alpha… he thought. His heart started to race. He thought about the empty tent next door. He thought about how Frank was not on the rescue mission. Brynn and Heart continued to ignore the conversation.

"You mean…" Henry started. "You mean… You killed Alpha?" Saba slowly nodded her head, staring down at her boots. Henry stood up. His hands trembling in anger. "I've got to talk to Frank," he said. Henry pushed passed Saba and Walsh and made his way to the entrance of the tent. As he reached for the zipper, it opened, and Frank Simmons came back inside. Henry stood there motionless. He stared at Frank, searching for some consoling words, but only managed a blank stare and a slight nod.

Simmons took off his coat and placed his M14 in the rifle rack. He placed his hand on Henry's shoulder and returned the nod. "It's okay Henry. Really. I just struggle with the story every now and then," he said. He made his way back to his cot and sat down on the end. The fabric of the old military cots groaned as it stretched under his weight. "Besides, after Almasi tried to have them executed and they helped get you back, I'd say we're okay," he said as he smiled at Saba. Henry stood by the entrance, still trying to take it all in.

"After the Penn State OP we reported back to Almasi. We heard about an attempt on his life," said Saba. She turned to face Henry. "He thought it was us," her voice cracked. "He thought we betrayed him by joining the Federation. That's why he kept you prisoner," she said, making eye contact with Henry. "He thought you would crack and give us up."

"So how did you end up here?" Henry asked.

"Prick tried to lock us up," Walsh said as he sat down on his new cot. The one that used to belong to Ahmed. "He told us you were there in the cells and he would make us watch your execution," he said. Henry made his way back over to his bed space and sat down next to Nella. He was still trying to piece it all together. His thoughts swirled through his head like a tornado. He told them about his first days in captivity and how the General was beating him for information on their location and how he thought he was working with them. He still had a bruised jaw to show for it. Saba explained that the two of them fled to F.O.B. Seven Springs and surrendered with the hope that the information of Henry's location would keep them safe.

Brynn had finished cleaning her MP-5 and joined in the conversation. She told Henry that they offered to lead the rescue mission since they knew the layout of the cellblock. "They were held as POW's in Seven Springs for a month until we heard about them," she said. "Once we had Colonel Howard on board we just needed to wait for a perfect time to move," said Brynn. Henry was listening intently, as though he were a child listing to his grandfather's old stories.

Walsh explained that there were reports of a massive force moving out of Pittsburgh, so they scouted the area for a few days and then moved in. "Easy peasy," he said, grinning through his beard.

"Where was the force headed?" Henry asked.

"Penn State. There has been non-stop fighting there for weeks now," Heart chimed in.

Henry started to feel overwhelmed again. He was still exhausted really wanted to get some more sleep. He glanced around the tent, taking it all in. Saba patted him on the shoulder and moved over to her cot. Tremblay's cot. Henry laid down. Time to rest, he thought.

EXECUTION DAY

Penn State University, Pennsylvania

Smoke billowed from multiple buildings, which casted a dark shadow across the skyline. Nearby gunfire echoed off the surrounding University buildings. The once beautiful historic buildings of Penn State University were now decrepit and derelict. Braden Murphy smiled and watched through a recently cleaned window of one of the few undamaged buildings. He watched as NBF troops lined up and executed four Sabre soldiers. The shots rang out, scaring a nearby flock of crows from their perch. The soldiers, tied to posts staked into the lawn of the Old Main building, hung lifelessly by the ropes that lashed them. Braden's smile grew wider. Four more Sabre soldiers emerged from the Old Main building. Led onto the lawn by NBF troops and lashed up to the blood-stained posts. They trembled and begged as the NBF troops took their firing positions. "I'll ask again…" Braden grumbled, "Where is this 'Rapier Squad' of yours?" He looked over at General Khalid Almasi who was staring through the window at his men. His eyes, bloodshot. His appearance, disheveled. His once pristine uniform was now ripped, and blood stained. He opened his mouth as if to speak, but no words emerged. Braden raised the handset of his radio to his mouth.

"I…" Khalid started. His voice hoarse. "I told you I don't know. I haven't had contact with them in months." Braden paused and stared forward through the window as Khalid trembled. He pressed the talk button on the radio and ordered his men to fire. Khalid flinched as the gunshots left his soldiers lifeless. Braden's smile started to fade as it turned to frustration. He pressed the talk button again.

"Bring out an officer," he ordered.

"I told you Braden. They've betrayed me. For all I know they are dead and rotting."

Braden lowered the radio handset and watched as a single NBF soldier escorted Major Hadad to the firing post. The Major had been General Almasi's most trusted confidant and a great friend. The soldier lashed the Major to the post and pulled his blind fold off. Major Hadd-ad began to shout something, but Khalid couldn't make it out. Braden shouted, "If they're dead and rotting, then who the fuck is killing my men!" His left hand squeezed the radio. Its plastic creaked and groaned. He drew his FN Five-Seven from its holster and pressed it to Khalid's temple. Khalid winced as the cold metal pistol barrel was driven into the side of his head. He sputtered out a few words. A mix of Arabic and English. Braden took it as he didn't know. He raised the radio to his mouth and paused, waiting for Khalid to answer. Nothing. He sighed. "Fire." Khalid flinched again at the sound of the shot. Braden hol-stered his pistol and ordered the two guards to take Khalid back to his cell. The cold metal barrel had left a perfect circle imprinted on the side of Khalid's head. He broke into tears as the two guards grabbed him by the arms and pulled him out of the room. His former confidant and friend tied lifeless to a wooden post.

***

The old wooden flooring groaned heavily under the weight of Braden's pacing. He moved back and forth staring at a large map pinned to the wall. The map showed the locations of the currently deployed NBF units in the region, the locations of recent battles as well as where potential enemy positions were. Next to the map is an index noting NBF unit strength and locations. He ordered a young soldier to pass him a marker. The soldier jumped from behind his desk and quickly moved across the room to hand Braden the marker. Braden grabbed it and began to tap the butt against his forehead. He stared intently at the map for a few moments. Thinking. His eyes darted back and forth, taking in the information. He flipped the cap off and it landed on the floor and rolled under the table behind him. A radio in the corner squawked, the static squelch pierced the silent room. Braden stepped forward to the map and pressed the black tip of the marker to the location of a new Federation outpost at a church where the Federation found dead members of a SOFREC team. He tapped it twice before sighing and stepping back. I don't have enough men to tackle the Federation now, he thought.

The newly named Camp Fishman has provided an unwanted presence in the Penn State area for Braden who had attempted to attack the Federation months before. Before the winter snow had set in, Braden mounted the NBF troops for an assault on the outpost while it was still under construction. He hoped that a fierce show of force and a massive blow to the Federation would be devastating enough to force a surrender. As his main force traveled down University Drive in a pre-dawn convoy, General Almasi and his Sabre forces ambushed them. Both sides suffered heavy casualties, with the bulk of the Sabres being captured, or killed. The NBF suffered such heavy casualties they had to return to base without completing the attack on Camp Fishman.

Braden looked over his troop strength index. "Two-thousand here and five-thousand back home," he said quietly in a whispered tone. The few officers standing by him felt the unease in his voice. They looked nervously at each other. A leader's unease has a way of affecting morale. The radio squawked again. The young soldier spoke quietly into the handset as Braden stared at the map. I can't attack them now, he thought. They are too fuckin' strong. He ordered the young soldier to inform all units to capture any enemy soldiers and round up any civilians in the area and ship them back to Boston for training.

FACE TO FACE

February 26th, 2021

McCalls Dam State Park, Pennsylvania

The snow crunched under their snowshoes as One Four Delta made their way through McCalls Dam State Park. The light of the moon sliced through the trees creating shadows that danced playfully over the mounds of snow. Henry Carson and Aaron Walsh lead the patrol through the State Park, making use of the thick brush. The cold air stung Henry's nostrils as he took a deep breath. Walsh raised a gloved hand and halted the patrol. Henry moved in close behind him, followed closely by Nella, Brynn, Simmons and Heart. They fell in and formed a tight circle, laying down in the snow and dense brush. Henry took a moment to admire the cohesion of his team. It was like a well-oiled machine. His mind started to briefly drift to Tremblay, but was snapped back to reality by a bright flash of light shining in their direction. Brynn flipped the safety on her MP5 from safe to three round burst. The light passed over them as the source, an NBF pickup truck, passed by on a trail about fifty metres from them. The well-oiled machine of a team tensed up ever so slightly. The truck rounded a corner and was lost out of sight. Only the whirr of the engine was left. But that too trailed off into nothingness. A few moments later, Henry slowly moved to a kneeling position and scanned the area. His heart was racing. This was his first operation since his rescue and he was more than a little nervous. He scanned the trees for movement through the sight on his new rifle. A black G36-C with an ACOG sight. The carbine was noticeably lighter than his old SCAR-L that Tremblay had given him. It felt almost like an airsoft gun in comparison. Henry's mind started to wander as he thought about that old rifle. How the last time he saw it was when he failed to pull the trigger and save Tremblay. Fuck. It's at the bottom of the river. A click snapped Henry back from his thoughts as Brynn flipped her submachine gun back to safe. Henry slowly stood up, followed by the rest of the team. He motioned for them to continue forward.

Nearly a week of heavy artillery and mortar fire from Camp Fishman had pulverized the NBF forces in Penn State. Intelligence received by an intercepted radio transmission indicated that Braden Murphy had ordered the surviving soldiers to retreat into the forest to regroup before heading back to Boston. The order came for Federation troops to clear the area and secure the former NBF Positions. Colonel Howard tasked One Four Delta with assisting two companies from the Tenth Mountain Division with sweeping areas of McCalls Dam State Park before breaking off and providing a recon of suspected enemy locations.

As One Four Delta pressed through the trees the sound of gunfire erupted in the distance behind them. The radio sprung to life with a contact report from a platoon in the Tenth Mountain. An ambush on an enemy pickup truck. Five enemy dead. One friendly dead. Was that the truck we let by? Should we have taken them out? He thought. No, stick to the mission.

They continued for another hour of slow travel through the trees and knee-high snow, stopping periodically to listen for enemy movement. Walsh halted the patrol again. Henry and Nella moved in behind them as the patrol took a knee. "What's up?" Henry asked. Walsh motioned forward to a flickering light about one hundred metres from their position. Henry scanned through his ACOG but couldn't get a good view of the light source. He moved back a few feet and tapped Frank Simmons on his calf. He motioned for him to move slightly out into the clearing and see if he could get a better line of sight. Simmons slung his M14 on his back and began a slow crawl through the snow. The light continued to bounce back and forth. It was a small orange glow that gleamed like a single eye of a demon. Walsh, Nella and Heart set up a firebase behind a large toppled over tree in case they needed the support on a quick exit if things went sideways. After all, things did have a way of going sideways rather quickly.

After a few minutes of crawling, Simmons was in position. He extended the legs of the bipod on his rifle after they sunk into the snow. He scanned the tree line ahead of the patrol and quickly spotted the source of the light. "Two armed soldiers," Simmons whispered into his personal radio microphone.

"Any vehicles?" Henry whispered back.

Simmons scanned the tree line again. "Negative. It looks like an observation post," he replied.

Henry whispered his plan over the radio. He quickly detailed how he and Brynn will move through the trees to the left and attempt to take the post quietly from the side, while the others provide cover. Brynn took a deep breath and nodded that she was ready to move. Slowly, Henry and

Brynn began to move around to the left. A tree branch snapped as it bent on Henry's chest-rig. They stopped dead in their tracks. The snap echoed through the quiet forest. God dammit, he thought. They quietly lowered to a kneeling position and Henry peered through his sight, scanning for movement from the Observation Post.

"You're clear," Simmons whispered over the radio. "Just take it slow."

Henry took a deep breath and glanced back at Brynn. The cloud of breath lingered in the cold air, illuminated by the moonlight. Brynn, crouched behind him, was ready to move. He motioned with his hand to carry on. They moved slowly and more deliberately. Henry tried to be more cognizant of tree branches and Brynn followed his footsteps almost exactly.

The trees began to thin out as they made their way further to the left. The clearing allowed them to move more quickly and quietly as they flanked the observation post. They finished their maneuver within fifty metres of the post. They could hear the two soldiers laughing over something. The light was their cigarettes bouncing around as they raised them to their faces. A rookie mistake, Henry thought. After a few minutes of waiting, he slung his G36-C across his back. It's too quiet out, even for a suppressor. He unsheathed his K-Bar Tactical knife from his chest rig and held it out for Brynn to see. The moonlight slid down the edge of the blade, creating sheen that made it look like diamond. She did the same. As they moved quietly, the whispered voices and laughter of the soldiers grew louder. Henry assumed they were making jokes about one or more of their officers. That's what he used to do when he was a grunt anyway. A light flashed as one of the soldiers lit another cigarette. Henry and Brynn were now only a few feet from them. The soldier's backs turned towards them. They were both sitting on a log behind a mound of snow they were using as concealment. In unison, Henry and Brynn each reached out and grabbed a soldier. Covering their mouths, they slid their knives into the soldier's ribs, forcing the blades through the layers of clothing. The muffled screams of the soldiers faded as their last breaths escaped through gloved fingers. "All clear, move up," Henry whispered to the team into his radio.

***

Clouds rolled in over the forest bringing with it a heavy snow. The thick snowflakes quickly blanketed the area. Braden Murphy patrolled around the centre of the hide as he oversaw the withdrawal of his forces out of Pennsylvania. His numbers were dwindling, and he needed to regroup with his main force in Boston before Federation forces catch up to them. His radio operator informed him that one of the two scout vehicles they sent out didn't return and they could not establish radio contact with them. They are getting close, Braden thought. His face distorted in a sort way that made it look as though he just finished sucking a lemon wedge. He ordered a nearby officer to increase the patrols and contact the Observation Posts for reports. The officer jumped out of the back of a large green truck and began ordering some soldiers about. Braden walked over to a small green tent, he opened the flap and went inside.

The inside of the tent was dimly lit by a small kerosene lantern hanging in the centre. Braden unzipped his white parka and unslung his AK-47 from his shoulder. He placed it on a wooden crate next to the door. "That's mine…" said Khalid. His voice was weak and raspy. He shifted in the cold metal folding chair. His arms bound to the backrest. Its metal joints creaked and groaned under his weight. Braden smirked, continued to remove his parka, and tossed it next to the rifle.

"It shoots nicely," he said, smugly. "Think I'll keep it." He pulled another chair up across from Khalid and took a seat. He leaned back, raising the chair off its front two legs. His hand gripped his holstered pistol. As he leaned in his chair, he stared at a battered and broken Khalid. His former friend. "You know," he started. "This could have gone a lot smoother." Khalid looked up at him, his eyes bruised and tired. The dark circles under them had their own dark circles now. Braden nodded as he took a deep breath. "Yup. A lot smoother. Why didn't you surrender your fuckin forces?" he asked. His voice reeked with an air of desperation and a hit of sadness. Khalid lowered his head again and let out a pained sigh. Braden grounded the chairs front legs and leaned forward, now almost face to face with Khalid. His breathing was heavy and angry.

"You won't win this," Khalid said. He raised his head, his nose inches away from Braden's. "The Federation will retake the East and you've burned your bridges in the West." Braden stared into Khalid's eyes; he grew hot as he filled with anger. His fist shot forward, finding a home in Khalid's stomach. Khalid let out a loud groan as the punch forced the air from his lungs. Without another word spoken, Braden Murphy stormed out, grabbing his parka and rifle.

***

The thick blowing snow made it easy for Henry and Nella to slip into the NBF hide undetected. They managed to crawl under an unattended pickup truck for cover while they waited for a two-man roving patrol to pass. All right, how do we do this, Henry thought. They didn't have nearly enough explosives between them to rig all the vehicles, and grenades would not give them time to escape. They could slash the tires, but destroying the vehicles was preferred. The guards had passed by, and Henry could see that Nella was having the same thoughts. She rolled onto her side and unsheathed her knife. She motioned for Henry to move to the large truck parked a few metres from them, and then she cut the break lines of the pickup. Henry squirmed out from under the pickup and moved over to the larger vehicle. An old Medium Logistics Vehicle that had seen better days. Henry crouched underneath and cut every tube and wire he could find. The mix of fluids quickly melted a patch of snow underneath the truck. Nella whispered over her radio that she had rigged an ammo truck with her explosives and set a remote detonator.

Suddenly, a muffled groan sounded out through the snow and wind. As fast as he could, Henry raised his rifle. He scanned for targets. Darting quickly from left to right. Trying to see anything through the dense wall of snowflakes. The distinct sound of crunching snow caught his attention. He swiveled to his left. Maintaining his crouched position, he aimed to the rear of the truck. CLICK! Henry flicked his rifle from safe to fire. The snow crunching grew louder and louder. A tall man, dressed in a white parka rounded the rear corner of the truck, an AK-47 in his hand. Its barrel pointed down at the ground. The tall man stopped dead in his tracks. He had seen Henry, but Henry had seen him first. TAK! The man dropped as a subsonic 5.56 millimetre round slammed into his chest.

Nella came running around the corner behind Henry, having heard the shot. "We need to move!" she said. "They would have heard that." Henry stood up as some muffled shouting rang out from nearby. They turned to leave the same way they snuck in but there were two guards moving towards them. Nella moved forward towards the man that Henry had shot. Form there she spotted a dark tent and made a break for it. Henry followed closely. She flipped the tent door flap open quickly and Henry sprinted in. The guards were almost at their old position by the truck.

"Uhhhhh… Is this who I think it is?" Henry asked, perplexedly. Nella turned to see her former General, Khalid Almasi, tied to a chair badly beaten and barely clinging to life. She stepped forward and pressed the barrel of her rifle to the top of his head. He looked up at her, his eyes widening as he realized who was standing there. The shouting outside grew louder. They've found their man. "Look, I hate to break up the reunion, but we need to get the fuck out of here," Henry said. He noticed a bundled-up pile of clothes that had been and tossed on top of a crate. He walked over and ripped a strip off a t-shirt. He used it to gag the flabbergasted Almasi. "Heart, we're heading back fast. We have a plus one. On our signal lay down fire," Henry said into his radio. Heart acknowledged as Henry cut Khalid loose from the chair. "Nella, bind his arms," he said. Both Nella Saba and Khalid Almasi stood face to face. Both trying to figure out what was happening. Neither of them moving. "Saba!" Henry shouted, snapping her from her daze. "Bind his fucking hands and let's go."

The three exited the tent and began scanning for soldiers. Khalid's legs buckled as he walked. They were weak. Saba grabbed him under the armpit and stood him up. They moved towards the tree line when a loud hiss screamed out, followed by a pop and bright light. The para-flare lit up the NBF hide like daylight causing them to stop running. Henry knew the best way to get noticed when there was a para-flare was to keep moving. They could see soldiers scrambling from tents and running around, no one knew what was happening. Fuck it. We've got to move. Henry turned around and pulled Khalid forward. Nella grabbed him by his armpit again and took off.

Henry never heard the gunshot. He dropped to his knees, his chest in a fire like pain. It was an excruciating, but familiar pain. It radiated from the centre of his chest and out through his arms. He had felt a pain like it before, but not for years. It took him a few seconds to realize the pain was from a bullet to the chest. A 5.7-millimetre bullet slammed into the ceramic chest plate of his body armor, shattering on impact. He gasped for air. The bullet had knocked the wind out of him. It still hurt like hell, but it was a hell of a lot better than the alternative. He could attest to that. Henry looked up to find where the bullet originated from and saw a tall man in all white staring at him, the front of his white parka stained red with blood. His right hand outstretched and holding a tan FN Five-Seven with smoke rising from the barrel. The man smirked and took aim again. Fuck. This is it… Henry thought. He closed his eyes and slowly took a breath. The pain in his chest continued to throb throughout his upper body. He waited for his life to flash before his eyes. He hoped to see faces of people he loved; his parents, friends like Jason Field and Joshua Maxwell, Brynn Parker, Frank Simmons, and

Jonathan Tremblay. However, nothing happened. A second felt like an eternity as he started to open his eyes.

Suddenly, a bright flash appeared, blinding him through his partially opened eyes. The force of the explosion engulfed the man in white in flame and knocked Henry backwards. He snapped back from his daze and quickly climbed to his feet. The ammunition truck that Nella rigged with explosives lit the surroundings up like the light of day. Sparks shot up into the sky as bullets cooked off and exploded in their crates. The NBF soldiers scrambled for cover, trying to figure out what happened. His radio sprung to life with Nella screaming to him to get out of there. Right! The signal! Henry sprinted through the snow as fast as he could. He ran passed two soldiers in a defensive position at the camps perimeter. They shouted in confusion as he sprinted by. It took them a few seconds to start to fire on Henry, but the mix of snow and flickering light from the fires made it hard to aim. Bullets whizzed and cracked by Henry as he made his way to Nella. The freshly fallen snow puffed up into the air as his boots plowed their way through.

More rounds zipped by Henry, this time, from the other direction. Machine gun fire echoed off the trees from Walsh's RPK. He slowly walked his machine gun fire across the camp, pinning the NBF down. Brynn, Heart and Simmons were more deliberate in their shots as they picked off soldiers as they ran for cover. Another truck in the camp exploded. Fire had ignited the fuel Henry spilled onto the ground when he cut the truck lines. Henry quickly caught up to Nella and Khalid who were just reaching Walsh's firebase position. Brynn fell in behind Henry as they passed by, followed by Simmons a few seconds later. Walsh and Heart continued to suppress the NBF troops as they scrambled to put out the fire that had spread to the tents. Like metal targets at a shooting gallery, the NBF solders toppled over by incoming fire.

Heart flipped his rifle to safe and tapped Walsh on the back. "Time to go," he said. He and Walsh began making their way back to the rendezvous point. Their position filled with spent casings, disintegrating link and snow blackened from their muzzle blasts. "Who's that dude with Saba?" he asked of Walsh.

"If it's who I think it is, he's getting a boot up his ass," Walsh replied. A few moments later, they reached the rendezvous point where the rest of the team were waiting for them. Khalid Almasi's eyes widened as he saw Walsh barreling towards him. A freight train with a fire red beard. Walsh's arm cocked back, ready to strike. Henry stepped in and caught the swing, taking the brunt of Walsh's weight and powerful punch. Using his right leg and Walsh's momentum, he leg-tripped Walsh, sending him tumbling to the ground. He clenched his teeth as the pain from the bullet to the chest resurfaced.

Henry stood over his grounded teammate and radioed the Tenth Mountain for extraction. They gave him a grid location, pick up time, and signed off. "We have one klick to the evac point," He said. "So, let's get moving and get our prisoner back unharmed." He reached forward and offered to help Walsh up with an outstretched hand. Walsh nodded and grabbed his hand, pulling himself up.

"You heard him," said Walsh. "Let's move."

ENTER THROUGH GATE 'D'

"Thanks to the intel gathered by One Four Delta in their capture of the Sabre's General, Khalid Almasi," Colonel Howard said as he stood in the war room. A large octagonal room dressed in black cloth covering the wood exterior. The walls were decorated in maps and computer monitors that displayed the concentrated war efforts of the Federation. It was the type of room you'd expect to see in the movies. When movies still existed. Soldiers worked busily on old laptops that were wired together with bundles of cables. The lack of highspeed wireless internet really made things difficult. "We have learned that NBF leader, Braden Murphy, may have been killed and his forces are retreating back to Boston," Howard continued. He paced back and forth at the head of the room as he spoke. His arms folded behind his back, which kept his posture rigid. A large screen on the wall behind him lit up with a map of Pennsylvania. It slowly zoomed in on their current position, then began to pan towards Pittsburgh. Two large green arrows moved along the map as it slowly panned across the state. The arrows were hastily drawn, most likely by a tech savvy soldier who remembered a thing or two about animation. Howard updated the unit commanders in the room on the current situation in Pennsylvania. "The Sabres are all but destroyed," he said. "We have two companies from the Second Canadian Division currently sweeping Pittsburg for stragglers." A few of the commanders let out quiet cheers.

Colonel Howard then turned the floor over to Lieutenant General Bob Epperson of the United States Army and Commander of the Federation forces in the east. Bob Epperson was a short stocky man in his early seventies. His uniform was in pristine condition with a perfect crease in the pants. He still wore his hair in a jarhead high and tight cut, although it was significantly greyer than it used to be. The large screen flipped to an old satellite image of Fenway Park in Boston. General Epperson pointed to the screen, wagging his finger at the playing field. The ball diamond in the old image was packed with people and surrounded by daily traffic. The green grass of the outfield popped right off the screen. "Gent's," he said. "Our next Forward Operations Base…" The room grew quiet, with the exception of a few whispers, as he continued with his plan.

As the unit commanders were leaving the room, Lieutenant General Epperson turned to Colonel Howard. "Colonel," he said. "You're to have One Four Delta sweep for Intel in the park." Howard nodded and left the room.

***

Three high explosive rounds burst forward from the barrel of a twenty-five-millimetre bushmaster cannon mounted on an M2 Bradley. The thumping sound they made punched the eardrums of the soldiers on the ground, causing them to cringe in agony. The heavy rounds perforated the concrete barricade that blocked access to Fenway Park, and detonated on the other side. Small arms fire snapped and whizzed by the Bradley as troops scrambled for cover. The NBF heavily fortified the intersections around Fenway with barricades, machine guns and RPG's. This was the last stand for the NBF force. Their numbers had dwindled ever since they retreated from Penn State. By the time the expeditionary force made it back to Boston, they were down almost five hundred fighters. Not to mention the nearly one thousand from the main force in Boston that deserted.

The Bradley's turret traversed to take aim and a machine gun position. The mechanical whir of the turret stood out over the sound of the rifle fire. Just as the barrel of the cannon sighted in on its target, an RPG screamed across Boylston Street from a nearby restaurant. A trail of dust and smoke filled the air in the street, leading back to the source of the rocket. Within a second or two, the rocket had slammed into the side of the Bradley, filling the armored vehicle with fire and shrapnel. Federation ground troops shifted their fire to the source of the RPG as another two Stryker Light Armored Vehicles moved up to provide cover. A soldier climbed out of the burning Bradley's turret, his back lit up in fire. He landed on the ground and began to roll about, not caring about the incoming enemy fire. The Bradley was now added to the list of destroyed NBF and Federation vehicles that lined the street.

The NBF machine gun position resumed fire, killing a group of soldiers trying to move up the street. A radio on the chest of a dead Federation soldier squawked as Henry hopped over her body. He sprinted for cover as rounds from a mounted PKM machine gun zipped passed him. He slid along the ground, taking cover behind a wall of sandbags that used to be an NBF defensive position. Heart dove for cover next to him. Heart screamed, "Jesus fucking Christ!" The machine gun had them suppressed. Henry looked around at the chaos. It had been nearly two full days of fighting now, and both sides had suffered massive losses. That was evident from this street alone. Henry counted five Federation armored vehicles and nearly fifteen NBF trucks burning in the street. Not to mention the countless bodies he could see. And that was just these two blocks. Rounds snapped all around them and sprayed dirt from the sandbags over their heads. Henry looked around or the rest of the team. He saw Brynn pull a wounded soldier to cover behind Walsh and Sabba who were firing on the NBF position. "We gotta take that gun out!" shouted Heart. Henry agreed and grabbed his radio's handset. He yelled into it for Simmons, and ordered him to grab a small team of soldiers and get to high ground. Another RPG tore through the air. It ricocheted off the side of Stryker closest to Henry and flew into the building behind them, raining glass and bits of concrete down to the street.

The machine gun fire stopped briefly. The pause allowing Henry and Heart to move. They sprinted into the garage of the building on their left, just in time. The machine gunner had finished his reload and began firing on them as they entered the building. The old mail sorting facility was near empty with the exception of a few mailbags and some boxes scattered around. A few unlucky soles never received their mail. They scanned quickly for threats then took a moment to catch their breath. While they did, four soldiers made their way across the street, drawing fire from the now reloaded machine gun. The rounds snapped and zipped by the open doors as the gunner aimed down his sights. A burst of three rounds found their way into the side of the fourth soldier. He dropped to ground, slumped over in the middle of the street. The three remaining soldiers made their way into the garage and moved to Henry's position to catch their breath. They looked back to their fallen friend as he lay motionless in the street. One of the soldiers, an older private, began to curse at the NBF through clenched teeth.

***

Frank Simmons pushed through the side entrance of the office building next to the machine gun position. Followed closely by a Sergeant and two Privates, both first class, from the Twenty-Eighth Infantry Division. The sounds of gunfire from the street rang out and echoed off the buildings as they moved they moved to the stairwell. Simmons pushed up the stairs to the open door on the first floor. He quickly leaned into the opening. No movement. He motioned for the others to keep moving while he covered the doorway. They continued up to the fourth floor, quickly scanning the other floors on the way. They reached the closed fourth floor and stacked up, with Frank at the rear. He was breathing heavy and he could tell the others were nervous. Frank would never get used to the stale smell of these buildings. They all reeked of death. "Alright," Frank whispered. "Let's clear this floor and we should be high enough to provide good support to the troops below." The four of them tightened their grip on their weapons and they each took a deep breath. Frank squeezed the back of the Sergeants arm, who passed the squeeze up. The soldier at the front of the stack quickly pivoted and kicked the door open with the heel of his boot. As fast as he had kicked the door open he moved out of the way to make room for the others to get by. The office floor was a large open office decorated in grey and blue cubicles. There was a long central walkway down the centre of the room. Along the right wall, a banner that once read 'Happy Birthday' hung loosely from the wall. The only light source was the daylight streaming in through the dirty windows. The air was just as stale in here as it was in the hall. Dust floated in the air and danced through beams of light shining in through holes in the walls.

"Contact front!" the Sergeant screamed. He fired two shots from his M4 Carbine assault rifle and ducked down behind a cubicle wall. The rounds thumped into a dry walled pillar next to six NBF troops who were setting up to ambush the advancing Federation forces on the street below. The soldiers quickly spun and returned fire, taking cover as they moved towards their attackers. Frank leaned out from behind his cubicle cover, quickly firing two shots into a soldier moving down the centre walkway. One of the NBF soldiers shifted her fire towards Frank. The rounds from her AK-47 tore through the cubicle walls sending bits of foam and particleboard soaring into the air. Frank, crouched down for cover, moved position and signaled to the Private next to him to move along the outside wall. Two rounds cracked through the air as they passed by Frank and found a home in the stomach and chest of the Private who had kicked the door open.

"Sergeant Thomason!" shouted Frank. "Let's give him some cover!" They both stood and fired a rapid volley towards the NBF, forcing them to take cover. Rounds from the Sergeants M4 took down one soldier who over shot his dive for cover. Bits of cubicle, glass and electronics bounced around and twirled through the air as bullets chewed up the office. Frank ducked to reload his rifle. He tossed the empty magazine on the floor and grabbed a full one from his chest-rig. The seven-six-two ammunition was heavy, but Frank was wishing he had restocked before entering the building. He was down to three magazines left.

The loud sound of automatic fire erupted on the left as the Private gunned down a soldier who was taking cover behind a pillar. He had used Frank and the Sergeants suppressive fire to move into a better position was able to catch an NBF soldier off guard. The three remaining NBF soldiers panicked in the confusion and attempted to withdraw, leaving them exposed to Sergeant Thomason on the right flank. He dropped two with well-placed shots as Frank took out the third. As the chaos ended and the debris from the cubicles settled, the wounded private let out a groan. He tried to sit up, but the pain was intense. "Sarge," Frank said. "Get him to a medic, Private Garcia can be my security." Sergeant Thomason lifted the wounded soldier up with help from Garcia and hoisted him onto his shoulders. He quickly set off back down the stairs. "Garcia," said Frank.

"Yah… Yes Sir," stuttered the Private.

"Check the enemy while I set up." Garcia nodded and headed to the nearest dead NBF soldiers and started removing the ammo from their weapons.

Frank moved towards the broken window in the middle of the building. Down on the street he saw Henry and Heart sprinting into an open garage door and rounds from a machine gun slammed into the ground behind them. He rested the folded bipod of his M14 on the windowsill and began scanning for targets. More machine gun fire erupted on the street as four soldiers sprinted to the garage where Henry and Heart were. Frank swung his rifle to the right and got a bead on the gunner. He exhaled and squeezed the trigger. His rifle kicked back as the round shot out across the street, hitting the gunner in the neck. He scanned through his rifle sight, moving back towards Henry's position. Movement in the restaurant across the street caught his eye. An old fifties style diner with red and cream décor. He swung back, just as a soldier in the diner fired an RPG. "Fu…" Frank started. A thick black smoke and debris surrounded him and Garcia as the RPG tore through the wall of the building.

***

Henry, Heart and their new team of soldiers pressed up against the ledge of the loading dock, looking for targets through the hole in the side of the building. The machine gun fire on the street suddenly stopped. Henry took the stoppage to his advantage, hopped the ledge, and moved towards the hole. Bricks and cinderblocks lined the floor around the opening making it difficult to move fast. He scanned for movement as he moved into position, crouching next to the opening.

Heart moved in across from him. Another RPG fired from the restaurant, but this time the NBF fired at the building across the street. That wasn't Frank, he thought. It can't be.

Heart used the lull in fire to move from the mail building to rear of the restaurant, followed closely by one of the soldiers. Henry and the other soldier followed suit and posted up behind them. "Stay here," Heart said to Henry. "Me and Bloggins here will toss a couple frags through the kitchen."

"My name is Upchurch," the Private said.

Heart stared at him for a moment before turning back to Henry, who nodded in support of the plan. The two of them quietly pushed into the rear exit of the restaurant. The kitchen was surprisingly modern for a fifties diner. It looked as though it had just been completed before the war broke out. A loud thump sound came from the dining area of the building. Now in the kitchen, Hear peered through the pass through window into the dining area. Two NBF soldiers were unloading a crate of rockets for the RPG. A few rounds of small arms fire ricocheted off the ground out front and whizzed through the building, causing the soldiers to flinch. Heart pulled an M67 fragmentation grenade from his tactical vest and held it out in front of him. Private Upchurch did the same. Heart whispered, "Three…Two…One." They both pulled the pin on their grenade and tossed them through the pass through window before sprinting back to Henry's position. The grenades landed with a thud next to the crate full of rockets. Muffled yells shouted out from the diner before the grenades detonated. The blast shook the building, sending smoke and dust in every direction. The explosion set off some of the rockets, causing them to launch out of the building like fireworks.

With the RPG team now neutralized, the two Stryker's began to move forward. They moved in behind the diner and into a large parking lot. Their large eight wheels moving over the parking space dividers with ease. The vehicles pushed their way through the parking lot, using their massive weight and power to move the old dead cars. They were followed closely by Brynn, Nella, Walsh and more foot soldiers.

Fenway Park was next.

Henry waved at Brynn, Nella and Walsh calling them over to his position, while the Stryker's and foot soldiers consolidated in the North end of the lot. Taking cover behind some parked cars, Henry explained the situation. "Simmons is gone," he said. "But we have to press on." Brynn's head lowered and she swore under her breath. A stray round zipped by, skipping off the ground next to them. The mounted machine guns on the Strykers hammered the front entrance to Fenway with sustained fire. "We're gunna need a way in," Henry said. "Anyone have an idea?"

"Yep," replied Walsh. "Be right back." He tapped Brynn on the shoulder and motioned for her to follow. The pair took off running back the way they came. A few rounds raced by as NBF soldiers fired on their movement down the alley. The Federation soldiers returned fire, igniting another firefight. Staying in cover behind the vehicles, Henry ordered Heart and Sabba to grab ammo from one of the Strykers. He covered them as they pressed up to the nearest Stryker, sliding over the hood of a shot up car as they moved.

Heart pounded on the rear door of the Stryker and shouted, trying hard to project his voice over the roaring drone of the engine and bursts of machine gun fire. The door swung open quickly and a young looking

Captain leaned out. In a gruff tone, he asked them what they wanted. "A box of five-five-six and some seven-six-two by thirty nine if you've got it," Heart yelled. The Captain shut the door and returned a few moments later with two ammo cans. He passed them out to Heart and Sabba and shut the door without saying another word. The two made their way back to Henry and Brynn, each carrying a can.

A loud roar came from the other side of the dinner, followed by the creaking and groaning of metal. An M1 Abrams tank rolled down the street with Aaron Walsh and Brynn Parker riding on the back. A large smile grew across Henry's face. He gave Walsh a thumbs up as the tank began its turn towards Fenway Park. The large tracks crushed the concrete parking dividers and cars in their path. Walsh and Brynn hopped off the tank and headed back to Henry. Once there, Walsh grabbed some ammo and began feeding the rounds into his weapons drum magazine. The M1 Abrams tank rumbled as it moved passed the team and took up a position on Yawkey Way next to a Stryker. The vehicle was a behemoth, filling up nearly the entire street. The barrel of the turret was nearly as long as the rest of the vehicle. The tank stopped moving next to an overturned delivery van and took aim at the barricade. As the turret moved towards gate 'D' of the park NBF soldiers began to scream and yell as they fled the position. The gate and ticket booth originally secured by a simple sliding fence gate was now heavily fortified with concrete barriers and sandbags. The tank paused, then, fired. The 120-millimetre tank round soared through the air and penetrated the first concrete barrier before detonating. The blast crumbled the barrier and exposed the entrance to the gate 'D' stairwell. The explosion sent debris almost one hundred metres in the air. Bits of concrete began to rain down as Henry and his team made a break for the opening.

MY COUNTRY NOW

Henry dropped two NBF soldiers with quick and well-placed shots from his rifle as he sprinted up ramp to the ballpark's upper levels. A loud burst of automatic fire from Walsh's RPK dropped another soldier who tried to take cover behind an equipment crate. The ramp was lined with rubble, bodies and splashes of blood. The Strykers on the ground level had provided suppressing fire for Henry's team and the results were a gruesome scene. A loud explosion erupted from the street level. Henry dove for cover behind another stack of equipment crates. Explosions were so common place now that he never had to think about his reaction anymore. Within a second of the detonation he would be in the air, diving for cover. This particular explosion however, came from an overturned delivery van that the NBF rigged up as an improvised explosive device on the street. They used it as a final defense measure and the resulting explosion had disabled the M1 Abrams tank right track and turret. Metal fragments from the van sprayed the surrounding area in every direction. A jagged piece ricocheted off the metal railing and tore into Hearts right thigh as he ran along the catwalk looking for cover.

He screamed as he fell on the hard, grey, concrete of the catwalk. Henry looked around as the chaos began to overwhelm him. His heart started racing. "William!" he managed to shout.

"Keep moving!" Nella shouted. "I've got him!" Two NBF soldiers turned their fire on her. Concrete fragments, dust and smoke besieged the air around her as she dragged Heart into the bathroom behind her. Once inside, she began to put pressure on his leg. Blood spurted out, creating a pool on the grey tile flooring. She grabbed a bandage from his tactical vest and wrapped it around the wound. A baseball diamond bathroom wasn't the cleanest place at the best of times, but it was safe for the moment, so it will have to do.

Brynn sprinted towards Henry's position. She fired rapid three-round bursts from her MP-5 at the last two NBF soldiers on their level. She placed all of her shots with a surgeon-like precision into the soldier's chests. She slid in next to Henry like she was sliding home and snapped him out of his shock. "Let's head to the broadcast room," she said as she helped him to his feet. They stood up and moved forward down the hall. That has to be the HQ, Henry thought. Thick black wires snaked through the hallways forcing Henry to mind his footing as he moved and cleared snack bars and drink stands. There was noticeably less resistance now in the building, and the gunfire from the street became the occasional muffled pop of a rifle or a machine gun burst.

***

A faint shuffling noise arose from inside the broadcast room. Henry quietly listened as Brynn and Walsh got ready to breach the door. The doors were heavy looking black doors, each with a single window. The windows had been painted over for privacy. The shuffling sounded like papers tossed hastily into a briefcase as though someone were in a hurry. Henry looked to Brynn and Walsh. They both wore a worried look on their faces. He had seen that look on Brynn before, but never on Aaron Walsh. But, he hadn't known him as long. Brynn signaled that she was ready. Walsh nodded. "Go," whispered Henry. Walsh stepped forward and kicked the door open. The force from the kick splintered the centre of the door, as it swung open. Henry and Brynn swiftly moved in as they had always done. They each cleared a corner. No movement. Walsh moved in behind them and slowly moved down the centre steps towards the window. The large windows were a giant curved gateway to the ball field. They once served as an area for broadcaster to watch the game and review plays, now, they served as a command post to a radical tyrant. The centre window was missing and ropes were leading out, tied to mounted desks. Walsh raised his weapon as a man stood up near the front. Henry swung his rifle towards the figure. The sight aimed in the centre of his back. "Hand's up and slowly turn around," said Henry. The man did as he was ordered and raised his hands; he slowly turned, revealing a badly burned Braden Murphy.

Henry lowered his weapon at the realization he had captured the presumed dead leader of the NBF. His mind raced with thoughts. Thoughts of the war ending. He turned to Brynn and motioned for her to secure the entrance to the broadcast room. She quickly lowered her MP-5 and moved to the doors. She struggled to close them. Walsh's kick and almost taken them off the hinges. Henry pressed his radio talk switch, the squelch echoed through the eerily quiet room. "One this is

One Four Delta," he said into the radio. "We have New Boston Front Leader, Braden Murphy in custody." No answer on the radio, just static.

"Didn't I kill you?" Braden asked, looking at Henry.

"Shut the fuck up," Walsh replied. He tightened his grip on his machine gun. He was staring at the man who was responsible for so much death. It took every ounce of his energy to not pull the trigger on his gun. No one would blame him if he did…

Henry glanced back to Braden and then tried the radio again. Still nothing. Radio static filled his ear as he tried a third time to radio the command vehicles. Braden smirked as Henry paced back and forth. He could see Henry's frustration growing. He stepped to his right. Walsh yelled, "Don't fucking move!"

"Why? Will you shoot me?" Braden asked. His tone reeked of sarcasm as he grinned at Walsh.

"Just give me a fucking reason."

"Uhhh, Carson?" Brynn said unnervingly. She was moving cables that bunched up during the door breach and discovered the rigged the computer desks with C4 explosives. Henry scanned the other rows and saw the same thing. Walsh looked to Henry to see what was happening, momentarily taking his eyes off Braden. Realizing his window of opportunity, Braden made his move. He grabbed a black remote device from the table in front of him and jumped out the window. Grabbing onto the rope in one hand, he slid down into the stands. He landed amongst the supply crates, generators and tents that had replaced the seats.

Henry sprinted by Walsh to the window. He watched as Braden made his way onto the playing field before stopping and turning around. Henry raised his rifle. Braiden raised his hand. Henry lined up his sight onto

Braden's chest. Braden squeezed the device.

The room instantly filled with thick black smoke. The bricks of C4 exploded, destroying the NBF equipment. The force of the blast knocked Henry out of the window. The fall was close to twenty-five metres, but as it was happening, Henry could have sworn it was nearly one hundred. He stared at the bright blue sky and fluffy white clouds as he fell, watching the black smoke from the explosion leak out into the open air. He was brought back to reality as he landed hard on a stack of green wooden supply crates and rolled onto the ground. His adrenaline was pumping as fast as his heart now, allowing him to brush it off as though it were a simple slip of the foot. He quickly got to his feet and sprinted after Braden not realizing he no longer had his rifle. The playing field, littered with tents as cables, created obstacles that Henry needed to avoid.

He rounded the corner of a tent and saw Braden turn to the right. Henry hopped over a small stack of ammo crates, nearly losing his footing. The old playing green field was muddy and brown, especially so since the snow had melted. He rounded the corner where he last saw Braden. As he did, Braden emerged from the tent and tackled him to the ground. They slid across the muddy wet grass and came to a rest against the base of a communications tower. Henry stood and turned to fight. His vision blurred as Braden landed a punch to the side of his head. Henry made a fist and swung hard. He connected with Braden's ribs. Braden leaned back and raised his foot. His muddy black boots had seen better days. He forced it forward with all his strength and kicked Henry in the chest, knocking him back to the ground. Henry groaned as he landed on his back and slid in the mud. He rolled onto to his stomach, gasping for air.

Drawing his pistol form its holster, Braden took a step forward. He was breathing heavily. Tired from the chase and short fight, his arms shook. He raised the pistol, aiming at Henry. Henry took a deep breath. As he did, he felt something in his hand just under the mud. Something metal. A piece of rebar! He grabbed it tight.

"I'll do it right this time," Braden said.

"Me first!"

Henry swung his arm as hard as he could. The piece of rebar exploded from the mud towards Braden. It connected with his arm and knocked his aim off, just as he squeezed the trigger. The shot from the pistol went wide and sliced through Henry's left shoulder. It just missed his fragmentation vest. Unfazed by the sudden gunshot wound in his shoulder, Henry burst up to his feet and sprinted towards Braden. He tackled him to the ground, knocking the pistol from Braden's hand. Straddling Braden on the muddy ground, Henry drove one fist into his ribs. Then the other. He drove his fits home like a boxer with an opponent on the ropes. He cocked a fist back. This time he aimed for the face. Time for the knockout. Henry's heart was pumping fast; he was so laser focused on landing his punches that he did not see Braden grab a fist full of mud. As he lowered his fist for a final punch, Braden swung his arm forward, tossing the mud into Henry's face. Henry fell backwards and squirmed as he tried to wipe the mud from his eyes.

He finally cleaned the mud from his face and through his blurred vision; he could see Braden Murphy standing over him. Braden had grabbed his FN Five-Seven pistol from the mud and pulled back the slide. A round ejected. He let the slide go. Another round chambered.

He was panting heavily now from the fight and was visibly sore from the punches he had just received. He staggered over to Henry. "This isn't how I die!" he shouted. He moved closer to Henry, now standing directly over him. "Twenty years of planning and fighting!" He took a deep breath. "And, I'm betrayed by my fucking allies." Strands of spit shot forth from his mouth as he yelled. He raised the pistol and aimed it at Henry's forehead. His hand trembled noticeably.

"This is my country now."

The sound of the shot echoed off the walls of the ball diamond. It was loud. Louder than Henry was expecting. And he had been shot at thousands of times. He slowly opened his eyes to see mud spray off Braden's chest as a round had penetrated his ribcage and perforated his lungs. Stunned, Braden staggered back. Henry couldn't move. He couldn't process what had just happened. He couldn't do anything. The shock was overwhelming him. Freezing his body like an ice sculpture.

Braden pressed his hand to the wound and examined the blood. He looked up and saw a soldier standing a short distance away. The barrel of the soldiers' rifle aimed directly at Braden. CRACK! The soldier fired another round into Braden's chest. This shot seemed quieter then the last. Braden tried to raise his pistol towards the soldier. CRACK! A final round.

Braden dropped to his knees in the mud. He tried to raise the pistol again, but he couldn't find the strength. His hand released the pistol as he died. His pupils began to dilate, giving a glazed over appearance, as though a had demon possessed him. He exhaled one final slow breath as his body slumped face first into the mud. The soldier moved forward towards Henry. His footsteps made a sucking noise as he walked

through the mud. "You good, Henry?" Frank Simmons called out. Surprised, Henry stood up. He grasped at his wounded shoulder. He had
thought Frank was dead. He had never been happier to be wrong.

***

Federation soldiers began clearing the tents on the field while Simmons and Henry sat and rested. By now, the ball field was buzzing with
Federation soldiers checking tents, crates and yelling around for assistance with things. The occasional nearby pop of a rifle would interrupt
things, sending the soldiers for cover. The outer cordon around Fenway
was working on clearing the buildings close by and would run into a few
NBF stragglers.

An Army medic dressed Henry's would after packing it with gauze.
Simmons light two cigarette and passed one to Henry. The medic made
a comment about their health but was met with unwanted gazes from
the pair. After a long drag on his smoke, Simmons told Henry that the
blast from the RPG had just knocked him out. He was woken up by
another large explosion from an IED and when he got himself together
he made his way into Fenway. He knew the plan was to look for Intel,
so he made his way through the building and found Saba carrying Heart
out to a casualty collection point. When he heard the explosion from
the top floor and made his way to the broadcast room. "I found Brynn
and Walsh a little banged up, but they're good," he said. "Then I saw
your dumb ass running across the field."

"Thanks."

"Don't mention it."

Henry placed his arm around Frank's shoulders as they watched the

154

soldiers work. Private Upchurch and another soldier grabbed Braden's body, placed it in a body bag and carried it off the field. Henry let out a sigh and hopped off the weapons crate he was sitting on. He wandered over to the tan FN Five-Seven pistol laying in the mud. He picked it up and cleared it. Quickly wiping it clean of mud, he stared at it. The worn-out tan body and black slide. He replaced the magazine and head-ed back to Lieutenant Frank Simmons. "C'mon, let's get some food."

VIVA LAS VEGAS

July 28th, 2021

Gass Peak, Nevada

The cool desert-mountain air began to warm up as the sun rose. It cleared a light fog from the hills as it arrived. The rise in temperature was quick in the desert, even at five-thirty in the morning. Henry Carson was perched up against a rock scanning the distance for movement. His ranger blanket tied to a nearby cactus, acting as a mix of camouflage and sunshade. He placed his binoculars down next to Simmons' M14 rifle and began to remove his scarf and Snugpak softie jacket. He was already beginning to heat up. As he packed them away in his small pack, Frank Simmons took a seat next to him. He passed him a canteen cup of lukewarm coffee. Henry nodded as he grabbed the cup and took a long whiff. The smell of coffee was always welcome. "Let's give it another fifteen and then we'll move out," Henry said. Frank nodded in agreement and began to square away his kit, so he could take over watch from Henry.

Brynn and Nella had just finished packing their kit when Henry walked back to the rest of the team. He sat down on his small pack and sipped his coffee. "What's the plan?" Brynn asked. Henry raised his canteen cup of coffee, and then took another sip. Nella laughed quietly.

Walsh and Heart strolled back from the truck where they had dropped their bags off. Brynn held her bag out to Walsh who walked right by.

"One man. One kit," he said. He slumped down on his rear, kicking up a small cloud of dust. He quietly screamed, "Fuck!" as he jumped back up. He examined the small cactus he had slumped down on, then kicked it with a bulky size eleven boot. Brynn laughed.

"Serves you right, ass," she said. She grabbed Nella's pack and made her way to the truck.

Henry packed away his empty canteen cup and cleared his throat. He pulled a map from the cargo pocket of his tan arid camouflage pattern pants and laid it out on the ground. The morning sun was bright enough now that no one had trouble seeing. "Alright," he said. "As you know, One Four Delta has been tasked with a recon around Las Vegas." The team nodded. "As of Twenty-two hundred hours yesterday we have been ordered to extend that recon into Las Vegas proper," Henry said sternly, his voice unwavering. He used his map pointer to show the movements of the Western Mountain Alliance forces in the area. "It's time to retake the west."

ACKNOWLEDGEMENTS

First, I would like to express my deepest gratitude to my wife Emily and my sister Cheryl. Without them and their support, this would never have been finished. Their assistance with edits made this less awful and the inspiration they showed, pushed me to make this real.

And finally, to the soldiers of the Princess of Wales Own Regiment and the Royal Canadian Regiment (past and present). The friendships I've made and the experiences we've shared will forever be held close to my heart.

ABOUT THE AUTHOR

D.S. Cannon is a former Canadian Forces member and a veteran of the conflict in Afghanistan. He served as a reservist with the Princess of Wales Own Regiment and then with the Third Battalion – Royal Canadian Regiment in Afghanistan. He retired from military service in 2013 a year after completing his post-secondary education and moved onto working in the administration field. He is the writer of 'A Procrastinators Blog', a personal blog in which he writes about daily life. His blog can be read at dscannon.blogspot.com.

Made in the USA
Middletown, DE
12 November 2018